Tetepu Takeover

A Podok Tales Adventure – Book 3

Chet Novicki

Table of Contents

For my favorite cousin, Linda-Jo Hubbard, with whom I share some sort of mystical connection that seems to transcend time and space.

Chapter 1

Will I never learn? I've been on Pode for less than a week, and already I'm up to my vox-box in mystery, intrigue, and other dangerous situations that normally would have me running in the opposite direction. The Podok curse strikes again, I guess. Perhaps I'd better explain.

I had come back to Pode to star in a flik based loosely on my adventures, in Hawaii, of a couple of years ago, when I rescued a visiting Prince Stee of Tetepu from criminals who had kidnapped him for his large, delicious, edible tail. While I'm not normally a flik star - actually, I've never even had a part in one - I was chosen by the producers to play myself because, and I blush as I say this, I'm sort of a hero in Tetepu, the largest country on Pode. Actually, that's not entirely true. I'm not sort of a hero - I *am* a hero.

And so I and my girlfriend, Donna Cabacungan, who, like me, is playing herself in the flik, and about 40 professional actors from Earth, had come to Pode to make this flik on a remote island some 400 miles from Tapu, the capital of Tetepu. After a brief stopover in Tapu to visit with the royal family and catch up on all that had happened since my visit here last year, we proceeded to Momasu, the island that was to substitute for Hawaii in the flik. Almost immediately things began to go wrong.

Our arrival on the island was greeted by the Podok equivalent of a hurricane - lots of rain and winds in the 70 to 80 mph range. The start of the flik was delayed for three days while the actors and technicians sat around in a large warehouse playing cards and checkers and mim-pat, waiting for the weather to clear. Most of the human actors stayed to themselves, not mingling with the Podoks, which caused a bit of a strain, but which wasn't all that surprising to me.

Because of the way they look - especially their big, sharp teeth - Podoks tend to be a little frightening at first. Even after you get to know them and find out they're really a very gentle, peace-loving race, their looks can be somewhat disconcerting, particularly when they flash those huge razor-sharp teeth at you. Actually, that's a smile.

And then Raz, Prince Stee's personal bodyguard, who was supposed to play himself in the flik, sent a message that he would not be able to make it. This briefly upset the director, who had to elevate one of the lesser Podok actors to what was essentially a co-starring role, and greatly upset me, for Raz was, among all the Podoks I'd met so far, my favorite. One of the three reasons I'd agreed to make this flik was the chance to come to Pode and spend some time with Raz. The other two reasons were, of course, credits and potential fame.

But the hurricane and the non-participation of Raz were nothing compared to what happened once we finally got started. On my very first day of work as a flik star, four huge - no, make that gigantic - policemen from the PNP, the Podok National Police, came to the set, talked to me for a few minutes, and then led me away. To those watching, it appeared I had been arrested.

At least, that's what everyone on the set thought. Actually, I was not under arrest, but had been secretly summoned by His Royal Highness, Emperor Da-mo Fen. The apparent arrest had been merely a subterfuge to get me away from the flik set without giving an explanation.

When I got to the palace, I found out why. Emperor Fen was in the palace infirmary, having suffered serious wounds in an attempted assassination attempt. While the official word was that he had been 'only slightly wounded' by one shot, actually he had been hit three times and had come close to dying. That he did not was due largely to the fact that the best doctors in Tetepu had cared for him and managed to pull him through one crisis after another.

And now he wanted to see me. As I walked down the long hall toward the infirmary, I wondered why.

The entrance to the infirmary was blocked by two Podoks in military uniforms - palace guards, I guessed. They looked up as I approached them, and I heard one of them - the senior one, judging by the amount of decorations on his uniform - say, quietly, to the other, "You can leave. I'll handle this myself." The junior guard immediately left, not looking at me as he passed me in the hall.

The senior guard then turned his attention to me. "Yes?" he said. "May I help you with something? Perhaps you're lost." He said it all with a smile, but it was an unpleasant smile. At least, in my opinion it was.

"No," I said, smiling back at him. "I'm not lost. I've come to see the emperor."

"Oh, I see. You've come to see the emperor, have you? And you would be?"

He was being snotty - he knew who I was. How many humans were there, wandering the hallways of the palace? "My name is Roger Denton," I said.

"No!!?" he said, feigning surprise.

"Yeah, I'm afraid so."

"Really? The Roger Denton they call 'the human who saves the lives of Podoks?'"

"Unfortunately, yes. That Roger Denton."

"And now you've come to see the emperor. How nice."

"Actually, he sent for me," I said, beginning to tire of this little game. "So can I see him, or what?"

"I'm afraid not," said the guard. "At this time, only members of the family are allowed in to see the emperor. Perhaps in a few days."

"But he sent for me," I said, protesting.

"I'm sorry," said the guard. "I realize you're kind of a big deal, a *really* important individual around here right now, but my orders come from the doctors, who, presumably, know what's best for the emperor's health right now."

"Yeah. Well, okay." You couldn't argue with doctors - everyone knew that. "Can you give him a message, then?"

"I'll try to see that he gets it."

"Tell him Roger Denton showed up, as he requested, but the guard outside the infirmary entrance wouldn't let him -"

My message to the emperor was cut short by the arrival of Prince Stee, who was coming down the hall, shouting, "Roger! Roger!"

I turned to greet him. "Hello, Your Highness," I said.

"Are you going in to see my father?"

"Well, I was -" I cast a glance at the guard "- but it seems the doctors will only allow members of the family in to see him."

"Nonsense. Who told you that?"

I looked at the guard.

"Why are you guarding the entrance to the infirmary, anyway, General?" Prince Stee said to the Podok whom I'd assumed was a guard.

"I'm, uh, just temporarily relieving the assigned guard so he can attend to some personal business."

"Couldn't you have found someone of a more suitable rank to take care of this?"

"It's just for a short time," the general said lamely. "I don't mind. It's an honor to serve the emperor."

"And where did you get that nonsense about only members of the family being allowed in to see my father?"

"That was my understanding, Your Highness."

"No, that was your *misunderstanding*," said Prince Stee. He sounded mad, which surprised me. I'd never seen him mad before.

"It's no big deal, Your Highness," I said.

"Come, Roger," Prince Stee said. "I'll personally escort you in. Unless General Noz-ti has further objections?"

"No, no, Your Highness. I'm sorry if there was a misunderstanding. Mr. Denton, please accept my apology for any inconvenience I might have caused you."

"Sure, sure. Forget it," I said.

We passed through the big door that led into the infirmary and stopped. "It's down at the end of the hall," Prince Stee said. "He's expecting you."

"You're not coming?"

"No. I have some things to do. Tell him I'll see him later."

"Okay. Listen, who was that guy? That guard?"

"That's General Noz-ti Pem. He's the Defense Minister."

"Really? The Defense Minister? Isn't that odd?"

"What?"

"That he's guarding the door to the infirmary?"

"Yes, I suppose it is. But he's an odd sort, anyway. Did he give you a hard time?"

"Yeah, a little bit."

"He's like that. He enjoys being unpleasant."

"I'd keep an eye on him, if I were you," I said. "There's something about him I don't trust."

"Oh, he's all right. He just likes to be in charge."

"I think that's what worries me."

Prince Stee patted me on the back, smiled, said, "Gotta go," and left.

I followed the hallway until it came to an end, at which point there was another guard. This time there was no problem, however. The guard opened the door to the emperor's room and said, "Go right in, Mr. Denton. He's expecting you." I did as instructed.

"Roger. Roger Denton," Emperor Fen said, as I entered the room. "Come." He held out his hand toward me.

He was propped up in a Podok hospital bed, which looks just like the kind of hospital beds we have on Earth, except I'm sure it has a hole or some sort of recessed area for the tail. I crossed the room to the side of his bed.

"Hello, Your Highness. How are you feeling?"

"Better. Much better, thank you."

"I'm glad to hear that."

"Do you know what happened?"

"Some of it. I talked to Prince Stee and a little bit to Empress Nememe. You were shot by two would-be assassins?"

"Yes. Two of them - one a Podok and the other, human."

"Human? Are you sure?" It seemed highly unlikely to me a human would be shooting at the emperor of Tetepu.

"I didn't see them," said the emperor, "but so I am told."

I wondered if I'd been brought here to defend my race. In any case, I felt impelled to do so. "Perhaps he was a member of some other humanoid race?" I offered.

"I'm told he had rather prominent ears," said Emperor Fen.

"Is that so?" was all I could think of to say. Prominent ears meant he was undoubtedly human. All the other humanoid races had only vestigial external ears.

"Do you know of PUFF?" said the emperor.

"I've heard of them. Podoks United, Fighting for Freedom. They want to overturn the monarchy and replace it with a democratic system."

"Yes. How do you feel about this?"

"Well, ..." I said, trying to think of some diplomatic answer to his question.

"It is a difficult question for you, is it not?"

"Yes, Your Highness. It is. As you know, I value your friendship, and that of your family, very highly. At the same time, ..."

"You believe in the democratic ideal," the emperor said.

"Yes. I do."

"I see."

"I do not, however, believe in the means these rebels have chosen to attain their goal. I believe in finding solutions through political means, not assassination."

"By negotiations, you mean?"

"Yes."

"That will be difficult, now that this has happened."

I had to agree with him on that point. Shooting the emperor didn't even make much sense from PUFF's point of view. As far as I knew, they'd always favored resolving the issue peacefully. I mentioned as much to the emperor.

"No doubt their position has changed," he said. "It looks as if they intend to force the issue."

"But PUFF is already an illegal group, and operates clandestinely, doesn't it?"

"Yes."

"So why would they do something that would put greater pressure on them? And probably result in a crackdown?"

"Obviously they think, with me out of the way, the government will be a lot less stable."

"You know, we're just assuming PUFF did this. It could be someone else."

"And who might that be?"

That was a very good question. Most Tetepuans seemed quite satisfied with the current system of government, at least, as far as I knew. I'd never heard of anyone or any group, other than PUFF, wanting to change it.

"I don't know," I said.

"I want you to do me a favor," the emperor said.

"Of course, Your Highness. Anything at all. I'm always at your service." As Confucius - or perhaps it was some other sage - once said - *When an emperor asks for a favor, a wise man says yes.*

"It will entail some sacrifice on your part. Are you sure?"

"Yes, Your Highness, I'm positive." I smiled at him, all the while hoping he didn't want me to babysit Princess Sesu again. "What would you like me to do?"

"I'd like you to join the investigation."

"The investigation?"

"Yes. Into my shooting. I want you to help the PNP find out who shot me and why."

"Me?"

Emperor Fen flashed his teeth at me. "Yes. You."

"But Your Highness, I'm a teacher. I don't know anything about investigating crime."

"No matter. I'll give you all the trained investigators you want. You tell them what to do and they'll do it."

I felt panic building in my chest. I knew absolutely nothing about the techniques of investigation. This was a task I could fail, and fail big time, and I'd already promised the emperor I'd do it!

"Your Highness, I'm perfectly willing to help you in any way I can, but I must point out I don't have any idea on how to go about this."

"You don't want to do it, then?"

"No, no, it's not that. But isn't this a job for the PNP? For professionals who do this for a living and, presumably, know how to conduct an investigation?"

"Don't worry about that. The police are investigating and will continue to do so. It's just that, well, one of these two would-be assassins is a human, and I thought it would be helpful to include a human perspective in the investigation."

"I see."

"And you are the only human I know, so I am asking for your help with this task."

"Thank you for your faith in me, Your Highness," I said.

"And that isn't all. Strange things have been happening recently. I'm not entirely sure who I can trust anymore."

"Strange thing?"

"Oh, just little things. I don't even mention them to anyone, for fear they'll think I'm becoming paranoid."

"An assassination attempt is certainly not paranoia," I noted.

"Yes, but I was referring to other, more subtle signs that lead me to believe there are those around me - close to me - who can't be trusted."

"Surely you don't mistrust anyone in your family?" I said.

"No. Not in my immediate family. I trust them. And I trust you, Roger, because you have earned that trust many times over."

"Well, thank you, Your Highness."

"Everyone in Tetepu knows you are the human who saves the lives of Podoks, and I know it most of all. You've already saved the lives of both my children, and now I'm asking you to help save mine. For if these killers aren't found and stopped, they no doubt will continue with their attempts to kill me until they succeed." Emperor Fen reached over and wrapped both long, prehensile fingers of his right hand around my wrist, and for a moment he wasn't the most powerful ruler on the planet, just a frightened, middle-aged Podok who didn't want to die at the hands of assassins.

"Of course I'll help you, Your Highness. I'll do whatever you want me to do. Or, at least, I'll try."

"Good." He released my wrist. "Is there anything you'll need?"

I thought about that for a few seconds. "Well, transportation, for one thing."

"I'll have one of my skimmers put at your disposal."

"I, uh ... I'm not much of a skimmer pilot."

"With driver. I'll let you have Sesu's new driver."

"She won't like that."

"Oh, I don't think she'll mind, since you and he are old friends."

"We are?"

"Yes. He is the one who helped you and my daughter when you were lost in the Valley of the Ancients."

"Dee-pok Slar?"

"Yes. You and Sesu were right. He was wrongly convicted by a dishonest magistrate. That magistrate is no longer with us, I believe." He smiled.

"Dee-pok Slar is Princess Sesu's driver?" I was having a little trouble grasping all this. The last time I'd seen Slar, he was living in a hand-built cabin in the jungle, hiding from a corrupt judge who was trying to put him in prison for a crime he didn't commit. And now he was working for the royal family!

"You'll find him most capable, I'm sure. What else will you need?"

"Well, ..." I paused to think about it, but not much came to mind. "I guess I'll need some kind of credentials, something that'll let me snoop around without getting myself arrested."

"I'll see that you get an Imperial Pass. You will be able to go anywhere I can go, do anything I can do. You will even be able to command the police and military, if you want."

"Really?"

"Yes. Really. What else do you require?"

"Well, ..."

"Don't be hesitant. Whatever you need, you shall have it. What is it?"

"It isn't a what, it's a who."

"A who?"

"Yes."

"Who is this who?"

"An-zo Raz."

"Prince Stee's bodyguard?"

"Yes," I said, mentally preparing to make my case should the emperor deny my request.

"Why do you want him?"

"Well, Your Highness, I hardly know my way around the palace, much less Tapu and the rest of the country. I'll need someone who's much more familiar with this country to guide me. And Raz is a handy

Podok to have around if there's any trouble. Also, I know and like Raz, and I'm certain we can work together to find out who did this terrible thing to you, and why." I took a deep breath.

"Fine," said Emperor Fen. "An-zo Raz will be assigned to help you. Anything else?"

"I'm sure there is, or will be, Your Highness, but your request has caught me by surprise. I need more time to ... assess the situation."

"Yes, of course. I understand. Fine." He pushed a button by his bed and a bodyguard - or perhaps he was a doctor - came into the room through a side door. I guessed he was a bodyguard, judging by the size of him and the fact the strange implements strapped around his waist looked more like weapons than they did doctors' implements.

"Mr. Denton will be staying with us for a while," Emperor Fen said to him. "Show him to the guest quarters and extend him every courtesy."

The big Podok bowed slightly toward the emperor, then held the door open for me to leave. I started out the door.

"One more thing," the emperor said.

I stopped and turned back to face him. "Yes?"

"You will report your progress directly to me."

"I understand." My audience with the ruler of Tetepu was over. I left and followed the bodyguard, if that's what he was, down the huge hallway toward the guest quarters, all the while wondering just what I was getting myself into this time.

Chapter 2

I sat on the edge of the bed in the sumptuous guest quarters, pondering what had just happened. In little more time than it takes to snap my fingers I was out of one job - flik star - and into another - special investigator for the emperor. In my heart, I knew this was the Podok curse, once again beginning to exert its influence on my life.

I was sitting there, feeling sorry for myself, when my stomach rumbled, alerting me to the fact my sole intake of food for the day had consisted of several cups of black coffee and a couple of chocolate chip cookies, and that this nourishment had occurred back on the flik set, a long time ago. Scanning the room, I found a buzzer near the head of the bed and pushed it. In short order there was a knock on my door.

"Come in," I called.

The door opened and a female servant, clad in the blue and yellow uniform of the household staff, stood in the doorway. "You rang, sir?" she said.

"Yes. Come in, come in."

She entered and closed the door behind her, then crossed to where I was sitting and stood in front of me. "How may I assist you?" she said.

"Well, ... what's your name?"

"I ... I am Kiki. Ten-zo Kiki."

"Is something wrong?" I said. She appeared to be very nervous.

"I am in awe of your greatness, Mr. Denton."

I laughed. "My greatness, huh?"

"Yes. You are the human who saves the lives of Podoks!"

"Yeah, well, maybe so, but right now I'm the human who's starving to death."

"You are hungry?"

"Extremely so, Kiki. Would it be possible for me to get something to eat?" Having stayed at the palace before, I knew the kitchen was open at all times, and even though I'd missed dinner, getting a snack would be no problem. I was just being polite.

"Yes, of course. Whatever you wish."

"Do you have hot dogs?"

"Yes."

"With buns?"

"Yes, I believe so."

"How about chili?"

"Both vegetarian and with beef."

I smiled. "Really?"

"Yes, really."

"Is this ... just ... just for me?"

"What do you mean?"

"That you have this kind of food. Is it because I'm staying here?"

"Oh, no. We always have a variety of Earth food on hand."

"Oh," I said, slightly disappointed. I guess it shouldn't have surprised me, though, to find the royal family was just like all the regular Podoks I'd met - they loved everything about Earth, including its food.

"Everyone loves Earth food," Kiki continued. "Even me." She smiled, evidently starting to lose her awe of me.

"How about Moon Cola?" I said.

"Oh, yes. Prince Stee's favorite."

"Great. I'll have three chili dogs - the beef kind - and a couple of Moon Colas, then."

"Right away, Mr. Denton."

It took about 20 minutes for my food to come. I sat at the table and chair across from the bed and wolfed down the chili dogs, all the while knowing I was courting heartburn and nightmares as I did so. The chili was pretty good - I've had better, but I've had worse, too. A lot worse.

I was taking my final bite when there was a knock on my door. "Come on in, Kiki," I called, assuming she'd come back to pick up my plates.

The door opened and a female Podok entered, but it wasn't Kiki. This Podok was dressed in jeans and a ragged T-shirt. "Hello, Roger," she said.

"Hello, Princess Sesu," I said, wiping my mouth with a napkin and scrambling to my feet. Princess Sesu was the one member of the royal family I'd missed seeing when I'd made my short visit after arriving in Tetepu. She'd been away on some sort of educational tour of the southern provinces.

"My, but aren't we formal?" she said.

I grinned. "Do you still want me to call you Sesu-wun?"

She smiled back at me. "If you like. But my crush on you has disappeared - you needn't worry about that any longer. Now we are just friends."

"That's good," I said. "So what should I call you?"

"All my other friends call me Sesu."

"Sesu it is, then. Is this just a casual visit? Or is there some specific reason you came to see me?"

"I thought we might talk."

"Sure. Have a seat."

She smiled and leaned back on her tail in front of me. I sat back down. "This is a terrible thing they've done to my father. I want to thank you for helping him."

"I haven't done anything, yet."

"I'm sure your assistance will turn out to be quite valuable."

"Well, you always did have a lot of faith in me."

"Yes, that's true," she said with a laugh. "When we were lost in the Valley of the Ancients, I always knew you'd get us out of there. And you did."

"This, of course, is something entirely different," I said. "I'm not a detective, and I don't know anything at all about how to investigate a crime."

"I'm sure you'll do just fine. I understand An-zo Raz will be assisting you?"

"It's more like I'll be assisting him."

"And I hear I'll be losing my personal driver," she said, pretending to pout.

"Yes. You're not mad, are you?"

"You know I couldn't be mad at you, Roger."

"That's great news about Slar - getting a new trial and all. And becoming your driver, too. That's terrific."

"Yes." She leaned over and said, in a confidential manner, "It's a much better job than driving a tram. It pays a lot more."

"I'll bet it does," I said.

We talked for nearly two hours, according to my watch, which was still set to Hawaii time. No sense in changing it - Earth time doesn't work on Pode, and I've never been able to adjust to the kind of timekeepers they use here. We rehashed our great adventure of the previous year, laughing and acting like a couple of kids, until at last I grew sleepy and began to yawn.

"I'd better go," said the princess. "I'm starting to bore you." She popped to her feet.

"No, no," I said. "I'm enjoying this. It's just that ... well, it's space lag, I guess. I'm still on Earth time."

"I have to leave, anyway. The beautiful young princess must have her beauty sleep." She made a mock curtsy and headed for the door.

"Thank you for the visit," I said, opening the door for her.

"You'll be seeing more of me, most likely."

"I'm looking forward to it."

She smiled at that. "I'm supposed to tell you that Raz will be here in the morning, ready to go to work."

"I hope he knows more about this kind of stuff than I do."

"Investigating, you mean?"

"Exactly."

"Well, you'll soon find out." She kissed me on the cheek and disappeared down the hallway.

I put my dishes on the small table just outside my room and got ready for bed. A rather large bathroom was attached to my bedroom, and in there I found toothpaste, a toothbrush, three different kinds of soap, a razor, shaving cream, and a pair of purple silk pajamas in my size. Normally - back in Hawaii, where it's warm at night, I mean - I sleep naked, but who could turn down a chance to sleep in purple silk pajamas? I took a quick turn in the mister, which is a Podok bathing device that sprays water all over you from very tiny nozzles, dried myself off and slipped into the pajamas. Needless to say, they felt great.

I climbed into the big bed, pounded the oversized pillow into a comfortable shape, then turned off the light and closed my eyes, secure in the comfort of my purple silk pajamas. Ten minutes went by. I was still wide awake.

Twenty minutes passed. I tossed and turned, and pounded my pillow some more. I was exhausted and I had a big day ahead of me, and yet I wasn't even a little bit drowsy.

When I hit the thirty-minute mark without any appreciable gains in the direction of falling asleep, I gave up, turned on the light, found the control for the video screen and turned it on. I surfed around until I found a news channel where they were discussing the attempted assassination, then propped myself up on the giant pillow and turned the sound up to a comfortable level, ready to digest the official version of the event.

A very serious-looking female Podok was leaning on her tail in front of an electronic map of where the incident happened - at a hotel in downtown Tapu, where a convention of tourism directors from around the galaxy was being held. Since tourism was, by far, the largest commercial enterprise in the galaxy, the directors of the Tetepuan Visitors Bureau had gone all out for the occasion, even persuading the emperor to show up and make a speech. The assassination attempt occurred as the emperor was being led through the hotel kitchen by his bodyguards, on his way to the convention hall.

As the serious-looking female Podok spoke, different sections of the electronic map behind her lit up, showing just where such-and-such thing occurred, or where someone was at a certain time. It was all very professional and everything seemed to be well-researched, but they were giving out the official story - the emperor was hit by one shot and was only 'grazed' by it. PUFF was suspected. The emperor was resting for 'precautionary' reasons and would be making a public appearance, to 'show he was all right,' in a day or two.

I listened for a while, but didn't learn anything I didn't already know except that the shot was of the solid-projectile type. Solid-projectile weapons - guns, in other words - are not much in use anywhere in the galaxy these days, except on Earth. Guns and ears. It looked as if a human was involved, all right.

After a time I began to feel drowsy, so I turned off the screen and just lay there, thinking, waiting for sleep to come. I wondered what Donna was doing, and if she missed me, and who they were going to get to play me in the flik. It seemed my flik career was over before it even began. I was pretty disappointed. I'd looked forward to being in the flik - it was something not many people could say they've done, and the pay, which I now would not be getting, I assumed, was excellent.

And now I was expected to solve - or help solve - the attempted assassination of Emperor Fen. This was not how I'd been planning to spend my vacation on Pode.

At some point I fell asleep and began to dream. I found myself engaged in a serious conversation with famous cartoon star Dinky Dogg, who just happened to be in Tetepu to open another of his galaxy-famous Dinky Dogg Restaurants, the specialty of which was

Earth-style chili dogs. Dinky was, as he always seems to be, in an upbeat, cheerful, positive mood. "You're gonna be a hero again, Roger," he said to me.

"I don't want to be a hero," I said. "I've tried it and it wasn't that great. Now I just want to live a quiet, peaceful life."

"But you're gonna be famous."

"I had a chance to be a flik star. Now, that was a fame I could've lived with."

"Ah, that's just make-believe," said Dinky, giving me a thumbs-down sign with one of his hands, or paws, or whatever they're supposed to be. "This is real life."

"What do you know about real life?" I said. "You're a cartoon."

For what I'm sure was the first time in his life - ever - the smile disappeared from Dinky Dogg's face and he looked sad. "I know. But if I'm good, maybe my fairy godmother will turn me into a real live dog."

"What? Isn't that Pinocchio?"

"I thought that was a card game."

I was getting a little confused. "No, that's pinochle," I explained.

"Oh," said Dinky. The smile returned to his face.

"So, Dinky, what are you doing here, anyway? Visiting me, I mean."

"Well, Roger, it's simple. I wanna be your sidekick, your faithful companion, your right-hand man, and help you track down the low-life scum who attempted to waste the Big Kahuna."

"The Big Kahuna?"

"Emperor Fen."

"I know what it means. But why are you talking like that?"

"Like what?"

"Like a twentieth-century gangster."

"We're cartoons," said Dinky. "We're supposed to talk funny."

"No, you're a cartoon. I'm a human."

"Then how can we have this conversation?"

He had a point there, and I was still thinking about it when, from his back pocket, Dinky whipped out a large hand mirror and held it up in front of my face.

"See?" he said.

I looked in the mirror. Sure enough, a cartoon version of myself looked back at me.

"So, can I be your partner? Your sidekick? Huh? Huh? Can I? Huh?"

I started to say something, but before I could, I was interrupted by a cartoon Raz, who appeared from out of nowhere.

"I am Roger's only partner being," Raz said. "No other partner is allowed." He looked to me for confirmation.

"That's right," I said to Dinky. "Raz is my partner. Sorry."

"If I take care of Raz, then can I be your partner?"

"What do you mean? 'Take care' of him."

In answer to my question, Dinky reached into that same, apparently-magical back pocket and pulled out a fencing foil. "En garde," he shouted at Raz.

I was just about to jump between the two cartoon characters when a garbage truck appeared, backing toward us, its warning beeper cautioning us to get out of the way. Beep, beep, beep, beep, it went. The next thing I knew I was lying there awake. It was morning, and the video screen was beeping and flashing me a wake-up call that said, *Breakfast is ready. We await you.*

I scrambled out of bed and into the bathroom. The first thing I did was look in the mirror, to make sure everything I'd dreamed was just that - a dream. Satisfied I was a real person, I started brushing my teeth.

My dreams are often strange, but this one was not only strange, but puzzling. What was Dinky Dogg doing in it? And why was I - and everyone else, for that matter - a cartoon? As I lathered up and started to shave, I tried to figure out the hidden significance of this dream, but, try as I might, I could come up with only one explanation that made any sense to me. Chili dogs.

Chapter 3

Breakfast was in the informal dining room. After wandering the halls, lost, for several minutes, I finally bumped into a servant, who escorted me there. Prince Stee and Princess Sesu were waiting for me, leaning on their tails around a large table.

"Good morning," I said, climbing into the lone chair at the table. I use the word 'climbing' in its strictest sense, because the seat of the chair was a good four feet from the floor, in order to accommodate the top of the table, which was about five feet from the floor. As I clambered up the side of the chair and into my seat, I felt like a little kid who has just learned how to get into his high chair.

"Good morning, Roger," said Princess Sesu and her brother, both politely ignoring my difficulties with the chair.

"Where's your mother? Isn't she going to eat with us?"

"No. She's having breakfast with my father, in the infirmary," said Prince Stee.

"Oh. Of course."

"But she sends her love," said Princess Sesu with a big smile.

I smiled back at her and helped myself to a sampling of the various foods which adorned the center portion of the table. A slice of ham, a couple of strips of bacon, scrambled eggs, toast and jam, and some black-flecked, green, squiggly things that both Prince Stee and Princess Sesu assured me were 'delicious' soon filled up my plate, and a servant filled up my extra-large cup with steaming coffee. As I dug into the delicious, fat-laden food, I couldn't help but wonder if the rate of heart disease on Pode had increased since they'd discovered Earth *cuisine*.

"What about Raz?" I said between bites of my breakfast, which, by the way, tasted extremely good. Especially the black-flecked, green, squiggly things.

"What about him?" said Prince Stee.

"When's he going to be here?"

"Oh, he's already here," said the prince.

"That's right," chimed in Princess Sesu. "He's having breakfast right now. In the employees' dining room."

"Oh. I see."

"We'll meet with him after breakfast."

I guess the look on my face must have reflected the way I felt, because the princess continued, "We really can't have him join us for breakfast, Roger. That's just not done."

"I suppose," I said.

"Commoners are not allowed to mingle socially with the royal family," said Prince Stee.

"What about me?" I said. "I'm as common as they come."

"Well, that's different," he said.

"Different, how?"

Prince Stee and Princess Sesu exchanged meaningful glances, and then the princess said, "Can I tell him, Stee?"

"Tell me what?" I said.

"Go ahead," Prince Stee said. "You'll never be able to keep it a secret, anyway."

"Keep what a secret?"

Princess Sesu turned to face me with a big smile on her face. "My father - after this is all over, I mean - is going to adopt you!"

"What?"

"He's going to adopt you. You'll be a member of the royal family, a prince," she said.

"An honorary prince," clarified Prince Stee. "You won't be eligible to become emperor."

"That's because you don't have a tail," said Princess Sesu. "You can't be emperor if you don't have a tail. But still, it's the greatest honor that can be bestowed on anyone. To be made an honorary member of the royal family is ... well, it's only happened three times before in our entire history, and never to someone who wasn't a Podok."

"I'm greatly flattered," I said.

"You can't tell anyone," she said. "Not yet."

"Yes," said Prince Stee. "You must keep it a secret until after the would-be assassins have been caught. Then my father will make an official announcement, and there will be a holiday declared, and you will be his honorary son."

"Unbelievable," was all I could think of to say.

After breakfast, Princess Sesu went off to take her morning class in how to be a proper princess, while Prince Stee and I went looking for Raz. We found him in a meeting room on the other side of the palace.

"Good morning, Your Highness," Raz said to Prince Stee as we entered the room.

"Hi ya, Raz," said the prince. "You don't have to be formal - we're all friends here."

"Thank you, sir," Raz said. I guess 'sir' qualifies as informal when you're talking to royalty.

"I really don't have anything to say to you," Prince Stee continued. "Everything you need to know is in the files Raz has. If you need anything else, just let me know. And keep my father informed of your progress. I guess that's it. You're on your own." And with that little speech, he started to back out the door.

"You're leaving?" I said. "Aren't you going to help us?"

"I can't," he said. "I have princely duties to attend to. Now more than ever, with my father not able to greet visiting dignitaries and such."

"Oh, yes. Of course. I didn't realize."

"Raz knows what to do. You're in good hands." He smiled and exited, closing the door behind him.

I turned back to Raz. "*Ma kit po an*, you old son-of-a-gun. How have you been?" I would have punched him in the arm but I wasn't sure he'd understand the significance of the gesture.

"Being good," he said with a big smile. "Always being good."

"Me, too. I'm good, too," I said. "It's good to see you, even if the circumstances are ... well, you know."

"Yes. Not good. But soon to be fixing."

"I hope so." I glanced at the table, which was piled with papers, folders, chipcards, and two computers. "What is all this stuff, anyway?"

Raz waved his hand, indicating the room. "All this our office is being."

"Oh," I said, a bit disappointed.

"Something wrong is being?" said the always-perceptive Raz.

"Well, it's just ... when Emperor Fen asked me to help him, I thought he meant, like, out in the field, interviewing witnesses, trying to come up with leads, that sort of thing."

"Yes, yes. Exactly. To be doing. But first, all known evidence is for studying. Then defectives are being."

"What?" I said. Raz had completely lost me on that last exchange.

"When studying evidence is to be finished, then defectives are being Roger and Raz."

"Defective?"

"Yes. To be defecting the crime."

"Oh, detective!" Actually, I was surprised I hadn't understood right away what Raz meant – I'd heard him use the word 'defective' before. Many times, in fact.

"Yes."

"Then we *are* going to get to go out and ask questions and stuff?"

"Yes."

"All right. So let's get going on the evidence that's already been collected."

Raz and I spent the rest of the morning going over the files and, at the same time, catching up on each other's lives. The evidence wasn't anything to get excited about, and neither were our lives. I personally would use the word peaceful to describe them, but I suppose, to some people, boring would be just as appropriate.

The PNP had spent a lot of time and energy tracking down and interviewing just about everyone who had been in the hotel the night the emperor was shot, but hadn't found out anything of real value. Those present that night fell into two groups - the ones who had seen something and the ones who hadn't. Of those who had seen, or claimed to have seen, some part of the assassination attempt, most agreed there were two shooters, one a Podok and the other a human. Most, but not all.

Some of those present in the kitchen claimed to have seen as many as four would-be assassins, at least one of whom had a drawn weapon but did not shoot. Backup killers, was the theory of one witness. Or perhaps it was the theory of the agent who wrote the report, I wasn't sure. Since I can't read Podok, everything we were looking at was being explained to me by Raz, and while I like the guy a lot, his insistence on speaking English - his own brand of fractured English, unaided by vox-box, I might add - can make things difficult sometimes. It is also, in my opinion, what gives him his unique charm.

While there were conflicting reports on just how many individuals were involved in the attempt on Emperor Fen's life, one thing stayed constant. No matter how many would-be assassins a witness saw, one of them was always described as 'human,' or 'humanoid.' Several witnesses claimed to have clearly seen external ears, which would make that assassin, without doubt, a human. Unless he was wearing false ears.

The rest of the PNP's investigation - so far, at least - had consisted of arresting known members and sympathizers of the banned group, PUFF. Podoks United, Fighting for Freedom. Cool name. I wondered if the Podok equivalent was equally creative.

Over 300 PUFF members had been brought in for questioning, and every one of them denied any knowledge of the attempted assassination. Several suspected leaders of the organization had been given lie detector tests, and all had passed. From what I could see from the evidence accumulated so far, the PNP had reached a dead end. No wonder Emperor Fen wanted outside help.

After a break for lunch - which we ate together in the employees' dining room - we went for a stroll around the palace grounds. Raz seemed especially thoughtful.

"A credit for your thoughts, Raz," I said to him.

"What?"

"A credit for your thoughts. It's an expression. You tell me what you're thinking, and I'll give you one credit."

Raz smiled, displaying those big, meat-ripper teeth. "One credit only? You are skating cheaply!"

"It's just an expression."

"I am thinking I do not know what to be next doing."

"Yeah, we're kind of at a dead end."

"You are not to be having ideas, Roger?"

"Well, I don't know. Someone must know something. Don't you have any contacts?"

"No. Guardbodies are not for to be contacts having, like police."

"You mean bodyguards."

"Yes."

"You know, last year I met a guy - a Podok, I mean. He was in prison for being a PUFF sympathizer, or supporter or something. His name was Mitz, ... Mitz something. Either I don't know his family name or I can't remember it, but he was the driver of the tram that took Princess Sesu and me to the hospital after we crashed in the prison yard."

"You are thinking this Mitz is something knowing?"

"I don't know. But we could go talk to him - maybe he's heard something. Even a rumor. It would be more than we have right now."

"This Mitz is still in prison being?"

"No, he got out a couple of weeks after I met him, I think."

"Yes, this is to be a good idea. To be talking to Mitz."

"It can't hurt. If we can find out what his family name is and where he is."

"Not a problem being," said Raz. "Come."

We went back to our office. Raz had his computer contact the warden of Tetepu Federal Prison, and when the warden was on the screen, Raz made an official inquiry as to the identity of the former prison tram driver known only as Mitz. In no time at all we had his full name - Lan-zen Mitz - and an address. Raz was right - finding out who Mitz was had been easy.

We decided to pay a surprise visit to Lan-zen Mitz, and were packing up a few things to take with us when a palace employee showed up with two Imperial Passes - one for Raz and one for me. Raz was extremely impressed. He held his pass - which was a small blue and gold chipcard with the official seal on one side and a hologram of Emperor Fen on the other - at arm's length and admired it, all the while saying, over and over, "This is not to be believing!"

"Believe it, Raz," I said. "We've got the power now. We could do anything - even take over the government, if we wanted to."

He gave me a curious look.

"It's a joke," I said.

"Not funny being," he said.

"Yeah, maybe you're right. Bad timing on my part."

We gathered up the rest of our things and headed out to the garage where the skimmers were kept. Along the way, we stopped at Raz's quarters in the bodyguards' barracks so he could change from his official uniform into civilian clothes. He chose jeans and a T-shirt, which is also what I was wearing. On the way out I grabbed a pillow from Raz's bed and took it with us. Raz looked at me with curiosity but didn't say anything.

"What about Slar?" I said, as we approached the skimmer garage. "I thought he was going to be our driver."

"No," said Raz. "Mr. Dee-pok is not for to be this day working."

"So who's gonna be our driver?"

Raz opened the door to the biggest blue and yellow skimmer in the garage, then turned to me with a smile on his face.

"For to be me," he said, and climbed in.

Chapter 4

I was halfway into the skimmer when a guard came hurrying up to us, shouting, "Stop! Stop!" I turned to see what all the excitement was about.

"What are you doing, Mr. Denton?" the guard said.

"Why, Mr. An-zo and I are borrowing this skimmer for a while. Don't worry. We'll bring it back."

"No, no. You can't do that."

"Why not?"

"This is one of the royal family's personal skimmers. You can't just borrow it."

"We have permission to use it."

"No, no, no," said the guard. "I have orders. Explicit orders from General Noz-ti himself. No one is to use the skimmers without his authorization."

The guard was being as nice as he could be, under the circumstances, so I decided to reply in turn. As pleasantly as I could, I said, "I have permission from the emperor, for whom I'm working. Isn't that at least as good as authorization from General Noz-ti?"

This piece of information seemed only to confuse the guard. "Well, ..." he said, obviously unable to come to a decision.

"Well, ...?" I said.

"The emperor?"

"Yes."

"Really?"

"Yes, really."

"I'm sorry, Mr. Denton, but I really need to see something official."

Up until this time, Raz had sat quietly in the pilot's seat, a quiet smile on his face as he listened to my conversation with the guard. Now he leaned over toward my open door and flashed his Imperial Pass at us. "How is this?" he said.

The guard's eyes got wide and the feathery rings around them expanded so far they disappeared from view. "Oh. I'm sorry. I didn't know. I'm sorry, Mr. An-zo, Mr. Denton. I didn't mean to delay you." He backed up and kept on backing until he went around the side of the building and was out of sight.

I climbed into the skimmer, a smile on my face. "I think I'm going to like that Imperial Pass," I said, at the same time stuffing Raz's pillow into the tail hole at the rear of my seat. The hole was so large I couldn't sit back without starting to fall into it, but previous experiences with Podok transportation had taught me to bring along something with which to block it.

"Yes," Raz said. "It is to be fun."

The inside of the skimmer was luxuriously appointed, with the finest woods and plastics used throughout. About what you'd expect from one of the royal family's personal skimmers, I guess. I finished fixing the pillow and settled back.

Raz had been watching me arrange my seat with obvious amusement. Now he fixed me with a quizzical look and said, "To be going?"

I nodded. "I'm ready. Yes. To be going."

Raz gave a few instructions to the skimmer and in a couple of minutes we were skimming high above Tapu, on our way to see Lan-zen Mitz, ex-prison-tram driver and former, and perhaps current, PUFF sympathizer.

"I am for to be soon retiring," Raz said, settling back into his seat and swinging around to face me. "This is why I am for a skimmer pilot learning to be. It will help me for to be a job finding."

"You're going to quit being Prince Stee's bodyguard?" I said, surprised. I couldn't imagine Raz doing anything else.

"Yes, to be quitting. Retiring. No more guardbody for Raz."

"What will you do?"

"I am not now knowing. Maybe for to become private guardbody."

"A private bodyguard?"

"Yes. Or maybe for to be a private defective."

I tried to keep a straight face, but the best I could do was limit myself to a big grin. "This will be a good experience, then. Working on this case, I mean."

"Yes," he said. Then, noticing my grin, he said, "Something wrong is being?"

"No, Raz," I said. "I'll bet you make a great private ... detective."

"Yes. Maybe so. Not for to be worried. Job finding is to be easy."

Ten minutes later we were parking the skimmer in front of a typical igloo-style house in what appeared to be a nice, middle-class Tapuan neighborhood. Since Pode, unlike Earth, has learned to control its population - roughly six hundred million Podoks inhabit a land area about equal to that of Earth - poverty is almost unknown, and I've never seen any neighborhood in Tapu that wouldn't qualify as at least 'middle class.'

We piled out of the skimmer to be greeted by the stares of curious neighbors, who were probably wondering what a royal skimmer was doing in their neighborhood, and who the two guys in the jeans and T-shirts were. For all they knew, we could have been two of the would-be assassins - after all, one of them was a human - who had now stolen one of the royal skimmers, but we'd only gone a couple of steps when someone cried out, "Hey! That's Roger Denton, the human who saves the lives of Podoks!" As I said, I'm famous on Pode.

Embarrassed, I waved to the neighbors, who were now pointing at me and whispering among themselves, as we made the long walk to Mitz's front door. Raz waved, too, and smiled broadly. He seemed to be enjoying all the attention.

We were still several steps away from the door when it opened, and there stood Mitz. Or, at least, I assumed it was Mitz, since this was his house. Basically, all Podoks look alike - to me and to other Podoks, as well, I'm told - but Podoks have an extra sense humans do not have, which allows them to recognize each other. It's similar to the sense of smell, according to Princess Sesu, who first taught me about it. So they can tell each other apart by using this sense, but I can't tell who's who until he starts talking to me, revealing both his voice and personality. Or hers, as the case may be.

"Mr. Denton," said the Podok standing in the doorway. "This is a surprise."

"Mitz?" I said, still not sure it was him. After all, I hardly knew the guy. A year ago we'd had a chance encounter that had lasted about 20 minutes, and during those 20 minutes we'd spent maybe two or three minutes engaged in conversation.

"Yes, it's me, Mitz. I am surprised you remember me. And my name. Come in, come in." He stepped to the side and held wide the door.

"This is my friend, Raz," I said as I passed him. "An-zo Raz." I briefly considered adding to my introduction the information that Raz was Prince Stee's bodyguard, then decided against it.

"Ma kit po an," Mitz said. "May you live 1,000 happy years." Raz returned the traditional Podok greeting, and the two of them went through that shtick where they make circles in the air with their hands, presumably to show they're not concealing knives or other weapons.

Mitz introduced us to his wife and young son, who was six, and we made small talk for a couple of minutes. Then the wife, Temma, excused herself and took the boy with her, leaving us to our business. There were no chairs, so I stood while Raz and Mitz leaned on their tails.

"I'll get right to the point," I told Mitz. "This isn't exactly a social call. Raz and I are investigating the attempt to kill Emperor Fen."

"Really?" Mitz said. "You don't think I had anything to do with it, do you?" A worried-looking smile crossed his face.

"No, Mitz, I don't. In fact, my impression of you - last year when we were talking, I mean - was that you would be opposed to this particular means of resolving the differences between PUFF and the current, legal government."

"Assassination, you mean?"

"Yes."

"You're right. I am opposed to killing the emperor, or anyone else, for that matter. I favor finding a peaceful solution."

"Good."

"But PUFF didn't do this."

"Well, that's kinda what we've been thinking, too. But that leaves us with a problem."

"What?"

"If it wasn't PUFF, then who was it? Who else would stand to gain anything from Emperor Fen's death?"

"I don't know," Mitz said. "I really don't."

"Would you tell us if you knew anything?"

"Yes. I would."

"So you have no idea who's behind this?"

"No. But I'm pretty sure it's not PUFF. I'm still in contact with some of them, and nobody knows anything about this."

"Listen, Mitz, think hard. This is important. The investigation is at a dead end, and we're desperate for a lead. Anything at all - something you might have heard. Even a rumor."

"Well, ..." Mitz said, "I did hear a rumor a little while back. But it was before the assassination attempt. Way before."

"What was the rumor?" said Raz, jumping into the conversation for the first time, and also speaking Podok. It was odd to hear him speaking good English - courtesy of my vox-box - for a change.

"Well, you know the camp in the Valley of the Ancients? The one they closed down last year?"

Raz said, "Yes," and I nodded. The camp had been a PUFF training facility, using the emperor's own private lands to conduct military-like exercises for the benefit of the organization's more radical members. Although no one had ever said as much, I'd always assumed the purpose of such training exercises - the ultimate goal - was the overthrow of the current government. Emperor Fen's government.

"The rumor was," continued Mitz, "a few of the members went back to the site long after it had been closed down, reopened it and held training sessions, supposedly for some secret project."

"You don't say," I said. "And -?"

"And ... that's it. That's what I heard."

"That's it? That's the whole thing?"

"Yes."

"You don't know the names of any of these members, do you?" said Raz.

"No, I don't."

"How about the secret project?" I said. "Any idea what it was."

"No. I doubt there even was one. If you ask me - and it seems you are - I think if it's true, if some PUFF members did go back to the camp and reopen it, it was probably just so they could run around in the woods and play soldier and tell themselves what mighty warriors they were. That's all that training camp ever was, anyway. An excuse for a bunch of middle-aged businessmen to play war games."

"You seem to know a lot about it," said Raz.

"Well, word gets around."

"Did you ever go there?" I said.

"No. Never. War is stupid. And war games are even more stupid. It never interested me. Besides, I was never a regular member of PUFF. They wouldn't have let me go there, even if I'd wanted to."

I switched the conversation to small talk. Mitz had been cooperative and answered all our questions, and I didn't want him to get the idea we thought he was involved, or responsible in some way for what had happened. We might need his help at some later date, and I wanted to make sure we parted on friendly terms.

After a few minutes of chitchat, Raz and I used the excuse of having to get back to work to end the visit. Mitz's wife Temma came out to say goodbye, and after an awkward moment or two, we left. A throng of neighbors had gathered around our skimmer, and I was forced to shake hands and explain to them that, no, Mitz wasn't in any kind of trouble and he and I were old friends and I was just paying a friendly call. They seemed to accept my explanation - I think the fact that both Raz and I were casually dressed helped to convince them.

I climbed into the skimmer. Before closing the gullwing door, I asked the crowd if they knew Mitz was a hero, that he'd had a role in saving Princess Sesu's life the year before. They didn't, so I told them a bit about it, and they were suitably impressed. As we lifted off, I could see them gathering around Mitz and Temma, no doubt demanding more details from their new hero.

Raz told the skimmer to take us back to the palace and we dipped to the left and headed in that direction. Flying the skimmer seemed to be something anyone who could talk could do - skimmer, do this, skimmer, do that. I wondered briefly why Raz had said he was 'learning' to be a skimmer pilot, but before I could ask him about it, he started talking about something else.

"What is Roger for to be thinking?" he said, speaking in English again. I really didn't mind Raz's fractured English. Compared to the flat perfection of a vox-box translation, which is what I got from every other Podok I knew, Raz's self-taught version of the English language was something of a relief.

"I'm thinking about that rumor Mitz told us."

"Yes. I am also this for to be thinking. You are believing?"

I shrugged. "I don't know. You know how rumors are. There might be something to it, or it could be nothing, just a ... a rumor."

"Yes," said Raz. "So ...?"

"It's not like we have a lot of other clues," I said. "I guess we have to check this out - it's really all we've got."

"Yes, to be checking out," said Raz.

"I think it's too late today," I said, noting the sun starting to tickle the horizon, "but tomorrow morning, let's get started early and go out there and check it out for ourselves. See if anyone's been camping there recently."

"This is good," said Raz. "Tomorrow to be going."

We were almost at the palace and the skimmer interrupted to ask for landing instructions. Raz told it to land in the same spot we'd vacated when we left, which reminded me I wanted to ask him about 'learning' to be a skimmer pilot, but, once again, before I could bring it up, he interrupted me with a question of his own.

"Roger, you are knowing this camp is where being?"

"Well ... no. Not exactly. Just that it's in the Valley of the Ancients somewhere."

Raz smiled. "This valley is hundreds of kilometers long being," he said. "Finding is for to be difficult."

The skimmer landed and we climbed out. "Maybe not. Does Slar come back to work tomorrow?"

"Yes," said Raz. "He is our driver being." He looked disappointed. It was obvious he would have preferred to be our skimmer pilot. Actually, I didn't understand why we needed a separate driver, anyway, since Raz could drive the skimmer. Maybe it was an insurance thing.

"Slar used to live in the Valley of the Ancients, back when he was hiding from the authorities. I'm sure he knows where the PUFF camp was."

"To be hoping," said Raz, without a lot of enthusiasm.

Chapter 5

Raz must have taken me seriously when I said we should get an early start on our trip to the Valley of the Ancients - it was still dark out when I got my wake-up call. I've never been one of those people who can just pop out of bed and be going full speed a second later - I'm more of a slow starter. I rolled over and stared at the ceiling.

This was all a waste of time, I told myself. We weren't going to find anything useful in the Valley of the Ancients - I could almost guarantee it. We'd go out there, poke around all day looking for clues, and come back not knowing any more than we already did. A waste of time ... and sleep.

I struggled to a sitting position and rubbed my eyes. This trip to Pode sure wasn't turning out the way I'd thought it would, back when I was on Earth. I wondered if Donna and the flik crew were having any fun. Strange, I'd hardly thought about Donna since I arrived at the palace. Too much going on, I guess.

Half an hour or so later, I was in the employees' dining room, barely awake, having breakfast with Raz and getting reacquainted with Dee-pok Slar, the Podok who had helped Princess Sesu and me when we were lost in the Valley of the Ancients last year, and who had been rewarded by being given the job of Princess Sesu's personal driver. He seemed happy to see me, and thanked me for my help in getting his conviction on trumped-up murder charges overturned.

"I really didn't have anything to do with it, Slar," I said, yawning. "The emperor's the one you should thank."

"Oh, I have," said Slar. "I've thanked everyone - Emperor Fen, Princess Sesu, everyone. And now I'm thanking you."

"Well, you're welcome," I said, not knowing what else to say. "I'm glad things worked out."

"Things have worked out wonderfully, Roger. I have this new job. Nami and I can be together again. We owe much of it to you."

I was starting to get embarrassed. "Tell Nami I said hello." Nami was Slar's wife.

"Oh, I will," Slar said. "She will be very happy you remembered her. She still talks about how you and Princess Sesu came to see her, to tell her I was all right."

"I take it you already know Raz," I said.

"Everybody knows Mr. An-zo," said Slar. "He is famous throughout Tetepu, just as you are."

Raz gave both of us a big grin.

"Oh, yeah, I forgot," I said.

After we'd finished eating, we headed out to the skimmer garage to pick up a skimmer for our trip to the Valley of the Ancients. The guard who'd hassled us the day before was nowhere to be seen, and soon we were standing in front of a line of blue and yellow skimmers - the royal skimmer fleet. When you're royalty, you need a lot of skimmers, I guess.

"Which one?" I said to Raz, knowing full well what he'd say in reply.

"The big one," he said, right on cue. "We are to be the big one using."

Raz and I climbed into the twelve-seater, but Slar stayed outside.

"Aren't you coming with us, Slar?" I said.

"No. I have told Mr. An-zo the approximate location of the PUFF camp. Or, at least, where I think it was."

"I see. And what are you going to do?"

"I will be driving Princess Sesu, as before." He stepped back as the skimmer motors began to hum.

"Well, we'll see you later," I said. I waved and then closed the door.

Raz gave instructions to the skimmer and we exited the garage, took off straight up, and headed out over the city toward the Valley of the Ancients. As soon as he had made sure the skimmer was following his instructions, Raz turned his seat around to face me.

"You think you can find this place okay?" I said.

"To be finding easy," he said with a grin. "I am coordinates having."

"What happened with Slar? I thought he was going to be our driver."

"Not to be needing. Raz is able for to be driving."

"What did you do, show him your Imperial Pass and tell him he'd been reassigned?"

Raz grinned again. "My friend Roger is psychic being."

"This is all probably a waste of time," I said, as we sped along toward the valley, our care and safety entrusted to our on-board computer and the network of satellites which kept us from crashing into other skimmers, planes, and large flying creatures like ro-nars.

"You are thinking clues will not be finding?" said Raz.

"Chances seem pretty slim to me," I said. "First of all, we're investigating a rumor. And even if the rumor turns out to be true, even if some PUFF members - some secret group within the organization - went back to the valley to train, it all happened a long time ago. Any evidence or clues they might have left behind is probably gone by now."

"Still to be checking must be," said Raz. "This is what defectives are to be doing - stories and rumors to be checking."

"I suppose," I said. "Besides, this is our only lead."

"Yes, other leads are not to be having."

"You know, even if we do find evidence PUFF, or some of the members, went back to the valley, that doesn't mean they were involved in the attempt on Emperor Fen's life."

"This is so," he agreed.

"They might have been, as Mitz said, just a bunch of middle-aged businessmen playing war games."

"Well, soon to be finding out," said Raz, looking at the skimmer's instrument panel. "Arriving is almost."

There was a slight bit of turbulence as Raz took over control of the skimmer, and then we were in the valley, skimming slowly along, following the river.

"To be memories bringing back, Roger?" Raz said.

I looked down at the river and the grassy meadows alongside it. I don't know what I was expecting to feel - some sense of nostalgia, perhaps, for the place where Princess Sesu and I were lost - but it didn't happen. Basically, I felt nothing. No bad feelings about the place. No good feelings. No feelings at all. It was just a river in a valley. Nice, but nothing special. I'm just not the sentimental type, I guess.

"Oh, sure," I lied. "Lots of memories."

"And now to be one year later again back. I am betting never this to be thinking."

"Yeah, you're right about that."

We passed the small waterfall that had almost cost Princess Sesu her life. It was the first place I'd seen that looked familiar to me. I pointed it out to Raz and told him how the princess and I ended up going over it, which elicited a chuckle.

We passed several more familiar-looking places as we continued up the valley. I pointed out where Slar's cabin had been - it had been torn down after he gave himself up - and I also managed to find the little campsite where Princess Sesu and I had spent several days trapped by torrential rains, and then we were into virgin territory. Slar slowed the skimmer to a crawl.

"This area is all new to me," I said. "The princess and I were never this far up the valley."

"You are knowing what looks this camp is having?" said Raz.

"No. No idea. There's not supposed to be any camp at all. Supposedly they tore it down and restored the area to its natural state, the way it was before PUFF built the camp."

"So what to be looking for?"

"I don't know - your guess is as good as mine. Anything that looks out of the ordinary, like it doesn't belong here, I guess."

"I am understanding," Raz said.

"I'll look to the right. You look to the left. Okay?"

"Yes. This is good."

"And, Raz -"

"Yes?"

"Don't forget to look where you're going, once in a while."

He flashed that I-could-eat-you-in-one-bite grin of his at me and said, "Yes. Not to be forgetting."

We continued following the river, with me scanning the river bank to the right and Raz checking out the other side, going slowly so we wouldn't miss anything. After just a few minutes, Raz said, "Look. Something is being."

I leaned over to his side of the skimmer. "What?" I said, looking out the window. "I don't see anything."

He pointed. "Over there."

I squinted, but all I could make out was a dark spot under some trees. "What is that?" I said.

"I am not knowing."

"Let's take a look," I said. "Can you set us down over there, to the left?"

"Yes. To be landing." Raz banked the skimmer slightly to the left and we began to descend. Unfortunately, we began to descend at a greater rate of speed than Raz had anticipated, and we missed the river bank by a good 10 feet, landing instead, with a great splash, in the river itself.

"Whoops!" Raz said with an embarrassed look. "This is not my plan being. I have been screwing ducks."

"You've been what?" I said, suppressing my urge to laugh.

"Screwing ducks. Is this not correct?"

"I'm not sure. What's it supposed to mean?"

"It is to be meaning a mistake to be making."

I thought about it for a few seconds. "Oh," I said, laughing. "You mean, *screwed up*."

"Yes," said Raz. "I am still for to be skimmer driver learning, and so sometimes I am screwing ducks."

"You'd better be careful," I said. "You don't want to get a reputation as a defective who screws ducks."

"Roger is not this incident for to be telling?" he said.

"No, Raz, I won't tell anyone."

"This is good."

Fortunately for us, the skimmer floated, so we didn't get wet. Raz managed to get us back into the air, and on his second landing attempt he got it right. We landed in the grassy field alongside the river.

"Much better," I said as we climbed out.

"Yes," he agreed. "Much, much better." We hiked across the field of knee-high grass toward the trees, which were grouped in a tight bunch of perhaps a dozen on a slight rise some 100 yards from the river. It didn't look as if anyone had been around recently - there were no trails or other signs of habitation. The field was full of farting fotods, those wonderfully-gassy creatures that had floated Princess Sesu and myself out of this valley a year earlier. As fotods are wont to do, they completely ignored us, forcing us to zig and zag our way around them.

There were other small animals around, too, although I didn't see them. They made their presence known through the rustle of grass and little scurrying sounds as we approached. This was different than last year, when there had been almost no animals in the valley. The PUFF trainees had provided much of their own food by hunting, and most of the animals in the valley had either been killed or driven away.

The dark spot under the trees turned out to be a wood pile. Somebody had piled up enough wood to keep several campfires burning for days. There were also other signs someone other than animals had been here. A piece of rope was tied around one of the tree limbs, for example.

"Looks like maybe some of the PUFF members did come back up here for training," I said. "Or maybe just for fun and games."

"Maybe not," Raz said. "This could original PUFF camp be."

"I don't think so," I said. "I think the original camp was on the other side of the river. At least, that's the impression I got from Slar last year. And Princess Sesu told me the original campsite was completely cleaned up and restored to its original condition by volunteers from the Young Podoks' Association Ecology Corps. You know those guys - they wouldn't have left stuff lying around like this."

"Hmm, this is so," said Raz.

"So let's assume this is it, that the rumor was true - some of the PUFF members sneaked back up here, to train or for whatever purpose, and this is their camp. Or what's left of it. Let's spread out and see if we can find anything."

"Yes. To be finding."

We separated and started searching. If others had been there to see us, I'm sure they would have concluded we'd locked ourselves out of the skimmer and had lost the chipcard that opened the doors. We kicked our way through the grass, moving fotods when necessary, looking for something - anything - we could call a lead.

It was Raz who finally found something. He called to me and I hurried over to see what it was.

"Look," he said, handing me a small, ragged, mud-smeared piece of paper with faded, not-quite legible writing on it.

"What is it?" I said, turning it over in my hand. "Can you tell?"

"I am thinking it is a name and address being. But it is not to be reading."

"You can't read it?"

"No." He took the paper back from me and sniffed it.

"Smell anything?" I said.

"No. Too old being."

"Well, save it. The PNP must have a lab or something that can figure out what it says. Let's keep looking and see what else we can find."

Raz placed the piece of paper into one of the small plastic envelopes he'd brought with him, wrote something on the outside of the envelope, and put it in his pocket. Just like a real 'defective.' I smiled, turning away so Raz wouldn't see.

We searched for another hour or so without finding anything else that seemed like it might be a clue or a lead, and then gave up. Whoever had been here had cleaned up the place pretty good. Now it was all up to that small scrap of paper. If we could find a way to read it, and if the writing on it turned out to be an address, maybe we'd have our first real lead. If not, well, we'd once again be at a dead end.

Chapter 6

It was well after lunchtime when we got back to the palace. Raz went into the kitchen and told the cook to make us something to eat, while I watched from the doorway. The cook started to yell at Raz, telling him to show up on time if he wanted lunch, but Raz showed his Imperial Pass to the guy, and 10 minutes later we were sitting in the employees' dining room, eating a meal fit for ... well, fit for an emperor, I guess.

After lunch, we headed over to the PNP headquarters building, in the heart of Tapu. We took a smaller skimmer this time. Raz claimed small skimmers were easier to handle in the busy air traffic of the downtown part of the city.

We parked behind the building, in a spot reserved for the commandant of the PNP. Raz thought that was pretty funny, and he knew nothing would come of it because the blue and yellow skimmer had the royal seal on it. And, of course, holding an Imperial Pass does tend to embolden a Podok.

The building - which was actually several overlapping, dome-shaped structures of traditional Podok design - had no windows of any kind and only one entrance. Or exit, depending on which way you're going. It looked to me like what we humans affectionately refer to as a 'fire trap.'

A uniformed guard at the front door asked to see our identification, and when we showed him our Imperial Passes he snapped to attention and saluted, slapping first his right hand to his left shoulder and then his left hand to his right shoulder, so that his arms were crossed upon his chest. Raz returned the salute, but I just gave the guy a little wave with my hand as we passed into the building.

There were three levels inside, about average for a large building in Tapu. Raz looked around for a bit, then took off toward a bank of elevators at the opposite side of the building. He seemed to know where he was going, so I followed him.

The lab was on the third floor. We had to show our I.P.s again to get in, and once inside, we got a lot of curious looks from the green-frocked technicians. I'm sure they were wondering how we got into this very secure place – especially, how I got in, since I wasn't even a Podok.

Raz had a few words with the Podok in charge, showed him the piece of paper he'd found in the Valley of the Ancients, and 20 minutes later we were skimming northward, toward the Tapu suburb of Sotem, with a name and address the lab had lifted from the paper.

"This is great, Raz," I said. "Absolutely great." My enthusiasm for what we were doing, which had been practically non-existent recently, had returned with the discovery of what I - and Raz, too - hoped was our first real lead on who shot Emperor Fen, and why.

"Yes, maybe good news being," Raz agreed.

"Do you know where this house is?"

"No, but skimmer is this address for to be finding."

The town of Sotem sits on a small plateau, perhaps 25 or 30 miles from the center of Tapu. It's a bedroom community, with no industry or large businesses. Most of its residents work in Tapu, but a few are employed in local stores and restaurants, of which there are many. There is also at least one bakery.

I mention the bakery because that is where the skimmer led us, to the *Original Sotem Old-Fashioned Bakery and Hot Beverage Shop*, right in the heart of the downtown shopping district. "Here?" I said, when Raz told me the name of the place. "This is the address on the piece of paper?"

"Yes."

"What about the name? What was the name?"

"Mem-so Kin."

"Well, maybe he owns the place. Or he could be an employee."

"Yes. To be hoping."

Raz parked the skimmer across from the bakery and went, on his own, to check things out, leaving me to sit and wait. He was gone for what seemed to me to be a long time, and during that period a crowd formed around the skimmer, trying to peer in through the one-way glass, which allowed me to observe them without being seen. It was all pretty amusing, especially when Raz returned and the crowd tried to disperse without giving themselves away as the nosy beings they were.

"So?" I said, when Raz was back inside the skimmer. "What happened?"

He grinned at me. "Raz is new bakery employee being."

"What?!!"

"Yes. To be in this bakery working."

"I'm confused," I said. "Didn't you go in there looking for this guy, Mem-so Kin?"

"Yes." Raz was still grinning, obviously enjoying stringing me along like this.

"And you came out with a new job?"

"Yes."

"So? What about Mem-so Kin?"

"He is former employee being."

"Uh, huh."

"Sometimes at this address he is mail to be receiving."

"Snail mail, you mean. Right?"

Raz gave me a confused look.

"From the postal service," I explained. I don't think they have snails on Pode.

"Yes."

"So, how often does he check to see if he has mail?"

"Maybe three or four days each."

"How does he do it? Does he come in, or does he call?"

"Both."

"So you're going to work in the bakery and catch him when he comes in?"

"Yes. This my plan is being."

"I hope you told the boss to tell him he has mail, if he calls."

"This I am already doing."

"Well, it sounds great. When do you start?"

"I am first to be skimmer moving, then to be working."

"Now? You're going to start now?"

"Yes."

"What about me? What am I supposed to do?"

"Roger is to be waiting," Raz said.

And that's what I did. I waited. Raz moved the skimmer to a spot behind the bakery where it wasn't visible from the street, and went to work. I stayed behind in the skimmer, amusing myself with various computer games, none of which I could figure out how to play, and by watching vids on the com-link.

After about an hour, an older Podok came out of the bakery and knocked on the skimmer window. He was wearing a white apron and he was carrying a box, which he indicated was for me. I pushed the window button and the tinted glass slid down into the door.

"Mr. Denton?" he said.

"Yes?"

"I am Zet. Ek-mon Zet. I am so happy to meet you."

I stuck out my hand. "How are you, Zet? I'm pleased to meet you, too."

He set the box down on the ground and took my outstretched hand in both his hands and pumped it up and down vigorously. "It is indeed an honor to meet 'the Human Who Saves the Lives of Podoks,'" he said.

"Well, thank you. Thank you very much."

He picked up the box and handed it to me through the open window, saying, "These are for you."

"Podok pastries?" I said.

"Oh, no. These are Earth-style pastries."

"You don't say." I opened the box and looked inside. Ek-mon Zet wasn't kidding - these were, indeed, Earth-style pastries. And lots of them, too. I recognized eclairs, cream puffs, sugar cookies, a variety of muffins, and what looked like several slices from a custard pie. "Gee, I don't know what to say," I said. "Thanks a lot."

"It is my pleasure," Zet said.

"I take it you own this bakery?"

"Yes. It is a family bakery - my wife and two sons also work with me."

"Well, thank them for me. I appreciate this."

Zet made a little bow and went back inside through the bakery's back door. I dug into the pastries, putting away two eclairs, all the sugar cookies, and a slice of what was, indeed, custard pie, washing it all down with spring water from the skimmer's mini-bar. All the pastries were delicious - I was impressed with the authentic Earth-like taste Zet had managed to achieve, especially since I knew he had done it using mostly imitation ingredients.

I guess pigging out on the pastries, combined with the boredom of having nothing to do but wait, made me sleepy, because the next thing I knew Raz was shaking me awake. It was dark out, the bakery was closed, and it was time to return to the castle.

"No luck, huh?" I said.

"No," said Raz.

"So, what's next?"

"Roger is hungry being?"

I looked down at my swollen stomach and my loosened belt and my jeans with the top two buttons open and said, "Uh, no. Not hungry."

"Then home for to be going, tomorrow for to be this place returning."

"We're coming back tomorrow?"

"Yes. Until Mem-so Kin is finding, every day for to be returning. This is good, no?"

Since we had no other leads or clues to follow, I had to admit Raz's plan not only made sense, but was the only thing we could do. "Yeah, Raz," I said, "this is good."

As we lifted off into the night sky, I considered the possibility I might have to spend the next several days waiting in the skimmer. I wasn't looking forward to it, but there seemed to be no alternative if I wanted to be on hand when our suspect was captured. Of course, if I'd wanted to, I could have worked in the bakery, too, or in any of the surrounding stores. After all, I had an Imperial Pass, just like Raz. But having a human hanging around would be so suspicious it would probably spook our suspect, which meant I was stuck waiting in the skimmer.

I leaned my head against the window and gazed out at the darkened landscape below as we skimmed along, heading back to the palace. Hundreds of bright stars twinkled in the Pode sky. One of them caught my eye and I made a silent wish upon it that Mem-so Kin would show up, and show up soon.

Chapter 7

For the next two days, Raz worked in the bakery. Actually, 'worked' is an inaccurate term to describe what Raz did, if what he told me was true. A more accurate description would be, 'leaned on his tail in the corner, ate copius quantities of pastries, and waited for Ek-mon Zet to give him a signal when our suspect showed up.'

As usual, I waited in the skimmer, which was parked in an alley directly behind the bakery. It wasn't so bad. This time, knowing I'd be stuck in the skimmer all day, I brought along a chipcard onto which I'd downloaded several books and games, as well as the notes for my own two books, which I planned to write ... well, someday soon, hopefully, since I'd already signed the contracts for them and accepted advances - advances I'd have to pay back if I didn't write the books.

So I had plenty to keep me busy. In addition, Ek-mon Zet, the bakery owner, kept a constant supply of bakery goods and hot, delicious, imitation coffee coming my way. Sometimes he brought these goodies out himself, and sometimes he let his wife or one of his sons deliver them. In this way I got to meet the whole Ek-mon family.

Two whole days went by with me waiting in the skimmer, whiling away the time playing bridge with the computer, reading, writing, and eating pastries. I ate so many pastries that when I weighed myself on the scale in my room on the evening of the second day, I'd gained four kilograms, or almost nine pounds! No wonder I was having trouble buttoning the top button of my jeans.

On the morning of the third day, we finally got the break we'd been waiting for - our suspect, Mem-so Kin, came into the bakery to check on his mail. I found out about it when Raz came hurrying out of the bakery and scrambled into the skimmer, saying, "To be going! To be going!" in an agitated voice. I waited until we were up in the air before questioning him.

"What happened?" I said.

"Mem-so Kin is to be arrived," Raz said, taking the skimmer up to about 500 feet and hovering there, above the bakery.

"So? Did you arrest him? Did you talk to him? What?"

"No. I am a better idea to be having."

"Uh-huh. And that would be -?"

"To be following," Raz said. He grinned at me, the morning sun glinting off his razor-sharp teeth.

"That is a good idea," I said. "But won't it be hard, following him in the skimmer. All these Podok vehicles look exactly alike, and they're all the same color, too." This was true, to an extent. All of the little electric vehicles ordinary Podoks used as transportation were remarkably similar in design - they looked like tall igloos on wheels - and most of them - I'd say over 80% - were white in color.

"No," Raz said. "This is to be easy. I am his vehicle starring."

He lost me with that one. "What do you mean, his vehicle starring?" I said.

"Look," said Raz. He tipped the skimmer onto its side so I could look down more easily. The sight of the ground down below us and the realization we were just hanging there, in the sky, held up by some principle of physics no one really understood, made my knees go weak.

But I saw what he was talking about. Directly beneath us, on the street in front of the bakery, a white vehicle was pulling out of its parking place. And on top of that vehicle was a big, black star.

"See," said Raz. "I am his vehicle starring."

"I see, I see," I said, holding tightly to my seat and wondering if the door - which was now directly below me - was securely fastened. I had a sudden flashback to a time in my youth when my grandfather had taken me to the Hawaii State Fair. A giant Ferris wheel had been one of the attractions, and I wanted to ride on it. Gramps was no fool, though, and refused to accompany me, so I went on it by myself.

Actually, that's not entirely true. I wasn't by myself. What happened was, when it came my turn to board the big wheel, the operator pulled me to one side and made me wait there until he found another *single* with whom to pair me. Eventually one came along, an older teenager who liked to rock the seat back and forth whenever the wheel stopped. And the higher up it stopped, the harder he rocked. By the time I got off the Ferris wheel that day, my knees were so weak I could hardly stand, and I've been afraid of heights ever since. It's not something I'm proud of, but I can't help it. I like to be on the ground.

Raz brought the skimmer back to a level position and the strength began to return to my knees.

"This star is also on our computer being," Raz said, tapping on the screen with one of his long, prehensile fingers.

I looked at the screen. On it was a map - presumably of the terrain below us, although I couldn't be sure - and on the map, slowly proceeding down what looked suspiciously like a street, was a small black star that ... that ... well, it throbbed. It got bigger, then smaller, then bigger, and so on.

"You tagged his vehicle," I said. "Very smart."

"Yes. Now following is for to be easy."

"Good. Easy is good, don't you think?"

Raz shot me a curious look, as if to say, "What kind of stupid question is that, human? Of course it's good." But instead he said, "Yes. Easy is good. Very good."

And it was easy, with that electronic star on Mem-so Kin's car. We followed him around for most of the day. The only trouble was, he didn't go anywhere or do anything unusual or suspicious. He went shopping for a couple of hours - we parked and Raz followed him on foot - and then he stopped at a restaurant and had a leisurely lunch. After lunch he went to a barber shop.

"This doesn't seem to be getting us anywhere," I pointed out to Raz.

"No," he said. "This is not good."

"I say, when he comes out of the barber shop, we arrest him, take him somewhere and interrogate him."

"Yes. This plan I am liking."

So we waited, hovering at about a thousand feet and a couple of blocks away from being directly above the barber shop, where we could see the front door clearly without tilting the skimmer too much from level. And we waited. And waited some more. Finally, after an hour or more had gone by and Mem-so Kin still hadn't come out, I began to worry.

"How long does it take to get a haircut, anyway?" I asked Raz.

"Not this long is taking," Raz said.

"You don't think he gave us the slip, do you?"

"Slip? What slip?"

"You know, got away. Maybe he realized we were following him, and he went in the barber shop and then went out the back door or something."

"No!" Raz sounded shocked, as if the idea our suspect might be the suspicious type never occurred to him. "This he would be doing?"

I shrugged. "I don't know, Raz. He's been in there a long time."

"Yes. I am for to be this checking." Raz spoke to the skimmer and we swooped down and landed just around the corner from the barber shop. My stomach made a separate trip, arriving a few seconds after the rest of me.

"Soon to be returning," Raz said, as he got out of the skimmer.

"Yeah, I've heard that before," I said.

But Raz was telling the truth this time - he was 'soon to be returning.' In fact, I didn't even have enough time to eat the last of the sugar cookies before he returned, and there were only three left.

"What happened?" I said as he climbed in beside me.

"Mem-so Kin is not being," Raz said. "He is haircutting, then leaving."

"Another door, huh?

"Yes." Raz was thoughtful for a few seconds and then said, "This is not good."

"Maybe he just had some more shopping to do, after he got his hair cut. And when he finishes, he'll come right back to his car."

"To be hoping," Raz said without a lot of enthusiasm.

"Sure he will. He's not going to leave his car here, is he? He'll come back - I'm sure of it."

We returned to our lookout spot in the sky, where we could keep an eye on Mem-so Kin's car while we worked on reducing the large amount of leftover pastries that had accumulated in the skimmer. Sure enough, after another hour or so went by, our suspect came back to his car, got in and drove away.

"Once again to be following," said Raz.

"You don't want to arrest him right now?"

"No. Street is too busy being. Too much at this time crowding."

I looked down at the street. Raz was right - traffic had picked up and there were more pedestrians, as well. Apparently the work day had ended for many Podoks.

So we followed the starred car of Mem-so Kin as it made its way from the downtown section of Sotem into one of the surrounding neighborhoods. Not wanting to take a chance on being spotted, we stayed a good distance away and relied on the electronic tag to keep us in touch. When at last the car pulled into a parking spot and parked, we knew it only because the throbbing star on our screen came to a stop.

"Mr. Mem-so is now at home being," Raz said.

"Yeah, looks like it. So now what?"

"Time to be arresting," he said with a big grin.

"All right. Let's do it," I said. "I'm ready."

"Yes. To be doing."

I had anticipated we would swoop down, land in the yard, arrest Mem-so Kin and lead him away in handcuffs, or leg irons, or a tail iron, or something dramatic like that. But that's not what happened. Instead, Raz instructed our computer to locate the nearest police station, and to connect us directly to the captain in charge. Once we had a secure link with the captain, Raz showed him his Imperial Pass and ordered him to dispatch two of his men to arrest Mem-so Kin and return him to the station, where we would meet them. The station captain was suitably impressed with the I.P., and said "Yes, sir," and "No, sir," so many times it was a little embarrassing.

I was gaining a new respect for Raz's professionalism. He had our man in custody - or soon would have - and we hadn't even had to get out of the skimmer. Hey, if you've got an Imperial Pass, you might as well use it. Right?

We killed some time eating a bag of brownies Raz had found stashed in the front somewhere, then headed over to the police station to see our suspect. I don't know how Raz felt, but I was sad - sad because the brownies were the last of our pastries and sad because we wouldn't be hanging around the Original Sotem Old-Fashioned Bakery and Hot Beverage Shop anymore. I had a sudden craving for an imitation blueberry muffin, made with genuine imitation berries.

Raz parked the skimmer in the station commander's reserved parking space. I wasn't surprised. Every time we were out in one of the palace skimmers and had to stop somewhere, Raz just parked wherever he wanted and dared anyone to do anything about it. Since the skimmer was obviously one of the royal family's fleet, no one ever did.

As we climbed out and headed for the building, I said, "Keep your fingers crossed, Raz."

"Why?"

"It's good luck."

"Raz is good luck to be needing?"

"Not just you. Both of us." I could tell he didn't understand, so I went on, "We need good luck with this guy, this Mem-so Kin. If he doesn't know anything, we're at a dead end."

Raz patted me on the shoulder. "Not for to worry, Roger," he said. "Mem-so Kin is something knowing, and soon to be telling." He flashed his teeth at me.

"Okay," I said. "I hope you're right." One thing was certain. If Mem-so Kin knew anything - anything at all - Raz would get it out of him. Of this I had no doubt.

Chapter 8

We created quite a stir at the police station. Raz smiled and waved at the officers and other employees as we were led to a back area, where the interrogation room was located, while I tried to keep a low profile. He really was much more comfortable with his celebrity status than I was. I couldn't help thinking that, after his retirement, he'd make a great politician.

Mem-so Kin was already there, locked in the interrogation room, pacing back and forth, a worried look on his face. We watched him on a screen in the next room for a short while and then Raz decided to question him.

"Turn off the viewing screen," Raz said to Ok-za Ton, the nervous-acting captain in charge of the station.

"I can't do that, sir," he replied.

"Why not? Is something wrong with the switch?"

"Oh, no. No, it's nothing like that. It's regulations."

"Regulations?"

"Yes, sir. Regulations. They require us to keep the screen active whenever a suspect is in the interrogation room, because we're required to record all interrogations, and it won't record if the screen is turned off."

"I see. Turn off the screen, Captain Ok-za. That's an order."

"But, sir -"

"Do you question the authority of the emperor?" Raz said. His voice, although coming through my vox-box - which isn't known for its ability to impart subtle inflections - sounded ominous and threatening.

"No, sir," Captain Ok-za said quickly. "Not at all." He reached out and pushed a button. The viewing screen went dark.

"Thank you, Captain," Raz said. He smiled pleasantly at the station commander, then turned to me and said, in English, "Roger is to be joining?"

"I think I'll wait out here, Raz." It's not that I'm squeamish, exactly, but the last time I'd seen Raz interrogate a suspect, he'd carved his name on the guy's back with a laser scalpel.

"Not long to be taking," Raz said. He opened the door and disappeared into the interrogation room, closing the door behind him.

For several minutes, all was quiet behind the door. I imagined Raz was explaining options to Mem-so Kin. You know, tell me what I want to know or else - something like that. I was just beginning to think Raz had convinced our suspect to talk when there came, from within the room, the sounds of raised voices. These were then followed by the sounds of a scuffle, which in turn were followed by more raised voices, then several loud cracking noises, and finally, a Pode-shattering scream. It didn't sound like Raz doing the screaming.

The police - there were a half dozen of them gathered around - looked at each other questioningly. They were obviously worried. Or hungry, perhaps. The two looks are very similar.

Several minutes went by in silence and then the door to the interrogation room opened and a smiling Raz exited, followed by a terrified-looking Mem-so Kin. "Good news," Raz said to the assembled policemen. "Mr. Mem-so has agreed to cooperate with us in our investigation." He turned slightly toward Mem-so Kin. "Isn't that right, Mr. Mem-so?"

"Yes," Kin said quickly. "Yes, I agree to cooperate. I'm glad to be able to help the government, and I do so freely and voluntarily, without any pressure being put on me."

"Mr. Mem-so is indeed a good citizen of Tetepu," Raz said.

Mem-so Kin smiled weakly at Raz's words of praise.

Raz turned to the station commander and said, "As you no doubt have surmised, Captain Ok-za, this is a top secret assignment which Mr. Denton and myself have undertaken on behalf of the emperor. I must swear you and all your fine officers to complete secrecy regarding all that has transpired here today, under the terms of the Official Secrets Act."

"Of course," Captain Ok-za said. The other officers mumbled their assent.

"You are familiar with the Official Secrets Act, aren't you, Captain?"

"Well, uh, I've heard of it, of course. But as to what it says, exactly, I'm not sure."

"It's simple, really. And it's easy to remember, too. It goes like this. *Anyone guilty of revealing secret information is subject to immediate execution.*" Raz had been smiling when he'd started speaking, but now, as he looked from officer to officer, no hint of humor could be seen on his face.

"Is all this understood?" Raz said.

Everyone understood.

"Good, then. In that case, Mr. Denton and I thank you for your help, and we'll be on our way."

"Uh, what about the suspect?" said Captain Ok-za. "What do you want to do about him?"

Raz looked at Mem-so Kin, who returned a nervous smile. "Mr. Mem-so, would you mind spending the next few days in solitary confinement?"

"What?"

"It has occurred to me that, cooperative citizen though you may be, the information you've provided would not be nearly as useful if certain individuals knew you had given it to me. To prevent that possibility from occurring, I'm afraid it will be necessary to isolate you."

Mem-so Kin looked quite unhappy about this turn of events, but he didn't say anything. Perhaps his recent experience in the interrogation room had imparted a certain wisdom about things like this.

Raz turned back to Captain Ok-za. "If you don't hear from me within 10 days, release him," he said. "Until then, I want him held here and isolated from all other prisoners."

"Yes, sir," said the captain. "We'll do it exactly as you wish."

"Thank you, Captain. I will remember your assistance in this matter."

Captain Ok-za smiled, displaying a fine set of extremely sharp-looking teeth. While all Podoks have sharp - very sharp - teeth, these looked especially sharp. They looked ... well, *dangerous* is the word that comes to mind.

And then we were out of there, Raz smiling and waving to the employees as we made our way to the exit. They all seemed to know who we were, and they smiled and waved back at us, and some even called out our names. These warm greetings made Raz even more ebullient, and he waved harder and started calling out short, encouraging phrases to the workers, such as, "Hey! How are you all doing?" and, "Keep up the good work." - things like that. I'm pretty sure, if Podoks had thumbs, he would have been flashing them the *thumbs up* sign with both hands. It was all thoroughly embarrassing, but I smiled and nodded to everyone as I followed along behind Raz. There wasn't much else I could do.

Once we were in the air and headed back to the palace, Raz filled me in on what he'd learned from Mem-so Kin. According to Kin, a small number of PUFF members did go back to the Valley of the Ancients for training. This group called themselves the Advance Corps, and they were tired of waiting - they wanted change now. Kin himself had spent a day at the camp, but had never gone back. In his opinion, the Advance Corps was a bunch of 'wackos.'

Although he could offer no evidence to support it, Kin believed that either some Advance Corps members had infiltrated the government, or some government officials had become members of the Advance Corps. Raz mentioned that rumors had been circulating for years that PUFF 'had guys on the inside,' and this particular piece of information might just be an extension of those rumors.

Kin also believed Advance Corps members were behind the attack on the emperor. Once again, though, he could offer no proof. He didn't even know the real names of the A.C. members, or how to contact them. He also knew nothing about the human who was involved in the attack, but offered his opinion that the human was really a Sarlanti in disguise.

"Sarlanti?" I said.

"Yes," Raz said. "They are our close neighbors being, and sometimes are trouble making."

"Really? I thought Pode and Sarlanti got along quite well," I said. After all, I had come to Pode on a Sarlanti ship and my fare had been paid for by the government of Tetepu.

"Sometimes well, sometimes not so well," Raz said.

It was an interesting idea - a Sarlanti disguised as a human. A little dye for his apple-red hair and a couple of fake ears and a Sarlanti would look just like a human - a sunburned human, to be sure, for Sarlantis had pale red skin, but the disguise would probably fool most Podoks.

"So what hard evidence did we get out of this?" I said. "Names?"

"No."

"No names?"

"Better than names being," said Raz.

"Better? What?"

"Mem-so Kin is to me an address giving."

"What address?"

"It is a PUFF safe house being."

"A what?"

"Safe house. When trouble is being, this house is for to be PUFF members hiding."

"I see. Well, that sounds promising."

"Yes. I am to be so hoping."

Raz told me where the safe house was, but, since I wasn't familiar with the surrounding territory, the address meant nothing to me. All I knew was it was about 30 kilometers outside of Tapu.

Our arrival back at the palace cut short our discussion of the Advance Corps, Sarlantis, and the PUFF safe house. What was on our minds now was food - dinnertime was long past, and neither Raz nor I had eaten anything since we finished the brownies from Ek-mon Zet's wonderful bakery. We headed for the employee's dining hall.

The cook didn't seem overjoyed to see us, but he fixed us some leftover ... something. I didn't know what it was - and I didn't want to know - but it was pretty good. Neither of us seemed to have much on his mind except his food, and the first three quarters of the meal were conducted entirely in silence. Or perhaps I should say entirely without talking, since the sounds of two hungry imperial investigators enjoying their meals did occasionally break through the quiet.

Finally, near the end of the meal, Raz spoke. "This is good," he said.
"The food?"
"Yes."
"I agree."
And that was the end of that conversation.

When we were done eating, we sat around discussing what our next move should be. Basically, our plan was to check out the PUFF safe house and see if anyone was there. If they were, we'd bust them, and if not, we'd get the PNP to stake out the place for us while we did ... well, I didn't know what we'd do, since we really didn't have any other clues or leads.

"So, do we do this tonight or tomorrow?" I said to Raz.
"I am thinking better is tomorrow. Better is daytime."
"Okay. Sounds good to me. Tomorrow, then. What are you going to do this evening?"
"To be sleeping," he said.

"Okay. I think I'm going to go to the infirmary and see Emperor Fen. He told me to report to him when I had some news, and this is the first time I've really had anything new to tell him."

"This is good," said Raz, "but Emperor Fen is not in infirmary now being."

"No?"

"No. Today is for releasing."

"So he's where? Back in his private quarters?"

"Yes."

"Well, I'll go see him there, then."

"Yes, this is good."

I said goodbye to Raz and headed toward the royal family's private quarters, which occupied one entire wing of the palace. I was feeling pretty good about the way things were going - it seemed we might actually solve this mystery and bring the would-be assassins to justice - and I felt sure the emperor would welcome the news. It might even help speed up his recovery.

There was a bounce in my step that hadn't been there since the emperor had asked for my help. I had a feeling - a strong feeling - all this would soon be over and I'd get to go back to the flik set. While my part had no doubt been filled by another actor, at least I'd get to be with Donna for the rest of our time here. Yes, things were definitely looking up.

Chapter 9

It took me a little while to find my way through the maze of corridors winding through the castle, but eventually I ended up at the entrance to the royal family's private quarters. A Podok of truly mammoth proportions - he must have been seven-and-a-half feet tall - and armed with the largest stungun I'd ever seen, stood guarding the door. I smiled my most winning smile at him as I approached.

"Hi," I said. "Roger Denton, here to see Emperor Fen."

"The emperor is not receiving visitors," said the guard.

"Oh. Really?"

"Yes, really."

"I'm not exactly a 'visitor,'" I said.

"No? What are you, then?"

"Well, uh, I'm here at Emperor Fen's request. He wants to see me."

"His Royal Highness wants to see you?"

"Yes. That's what I said. I'm here on official business, at the request of the emperor."

"My orders are to let no one in. Visitors, humans on so-called official business, whatever, it makes no difference. No one gets in until my orders are changed."

"Oh." It looked like I'd gone as far as I was going to go on this particular evening. I nodded at the guard and started to walk away. And then I remembered my Imperial Pass.

"Listen," I said, "did I hear you correctly? About no one getting in until your orders are changed?"

"That's right."

"Okay, then. Listen up. I'm changing your orders."

"You?" The guard looked at me with what could only be described as a sneer.

"Yes, me. I order you to let me in to see the emperor."

"By whose authority?" said the guard.

"The emperor's," I said, and showed him my Imperial Pass.

If I thought I was going to dazzle the guard and have him apologizing to me, I was wrong. He did, however, lose the sneer. It was replaced by a look of confusion.

"An Imperial Pass?" he said. "I don't think that gives you the right to change my orders."

"You don't, huh? I represent the emperor. An order from me is the same as an order from him. Are you refusing an order from the emperor?"

"Well, ..."

"Look, I'll make this decision easy for you," I said, becoming genuinely annoyed with the guard's refusal to obey my order. "You either let me in right now, or I'll leave and return with 10 members of the Podok National Police, have you arrested and immediately executed in the name of the emperor."

"You can't do that," the guard said.

I waved my I.P. at him. "Oh, but I can. And I will. By the way, do you know how they execute Podoks who disobey an order from the emperor?"

"No."

"Slow roasting over an open flame," I said. This wasn't exactly true - in fact I had no idea how executions were carried out in Tetepu, or even if they had the death penalty for disobeying an order from the emperor - but it had the desired effect. The big, tough guard shuddered slightly and then stepped aside and opened the door.

"Go ahead," he said.

I reminded myself that gloating is unbecoming to the one doing the gloating, and could even be dangerous, especially when the gloatee is a gigantic Podok and the gloater is a puny, out-of-shape, 160-pound human. So instead of gloating about my small victory over the guard, I said, "Thank you," and passed into the royal family's private quarters. I made a quick mental note to also thank Princess Sesu, for it was from her I had appropriated the 'slow roasting over an open flame' line. It was her favorite threatened punishment for those who displeased her.

The door I'd just passed through led directly into a ... well, I guess it was a waiting room, although I'm not positive about that. In any case, it was a small room, with walls painted a bright yellow and hung with abstract paintings. A table sat in the center, upon which were scattered some expensive-looking books. There were no chairs or couches, like you'd find in a waiting room on Earth, but since chairs were rare and couches nonexistent in Tetepu, I wasn't too surprised by that. What was surprising was that no one was in the room. I'd sort of expected to be greeted by a secretary, or a servant of some sort.

"Hello," I called out. "Is anyone here?"

No one answered.

I made my way through an open doorway, which led to a short, descending staircase of only three steps, which in turn led to a ... well, it looked like another waiting room, only it was twice as large as the first waiting room, if that's what the first room was.

"Hello? Emperor Fen? Prince Stee? Anyone here?"

Still no answer.

I wandered from room to room, calling out to anyone who might hear my voice. No one answered. I began to get an uneasy feeling. Someone - if only a servant - should be here.

I located what was apparently the royal bedroom, judging by the size of the huge, canopied bed. This room, too, was empty. If Emperor Fen had been released from the infirmary today, as Raz had said, this is where he most likely would be.

And then the answer came to me. It was simple, really - Raz had been wrong. Emperor Fen hadn't been released from the infirmary today, he was still there. As were the other members of the royal family, no doubt. I breathed a huge sigh of relief and realized I'd been holding my breath.

I backtracked my way out of the royal quarters and headed toward the infirmary. The huge guard who hadn't wanted to let me in was gone from his post in front of the door. I wondered if he'd gone to lodge a protest about having to take orders from a human. It was strange the way he'd insisted I couldn't go in to see the emperor, when all along the quarters had been empty.

Whatever. I was confident I'd solved the mystery of the missing royal family. If they weren't in their quarters, they had to be in the infirmary. Unfortunately, upon my arrival there, I found out my solution was incorrect. The infirmary was empty - no guards, no nurses, no doctors, and no Emperor Fen. What on Pode was going on?

Perhaps I was being paranoid, but it seemed to me something strange - something very strange - was happening in the palace. It looked as if the emperor - indeed, the whole royal family - was missing. Unless the emperor was just feeling so good he decided to take the family out for ice cream. Or pizza.

Yeah, right. Something strange was going on, all right, and I was pretty sure it didn't involve going out for snacks.

I decided it was time to find Raz and let him know about my suspicions. If I was wrong, well, I could live with the embarrassment of my mistake. But if I was right ...

I was halfway to Raz's quarters when I was stopped by two armed guards. One of them pointed a stungun at me and the other one advised me not to move.

"What's the problem?" I said.

"Roger Denton?" said the guard who wasn't pointing a stungun at me.

"Yes. That's me."

"You are hereby placed under arrest for your part in the attempted assassination of His Royal Highness, Emperor Da-mo Fen."

"What?!!"

"You're under arrest."

"But I didn't have anything to do with that! I was on Momasu Island, hundreds of kilometers away from here at the time, and I can prove it!"

"You'll have your chance to prove your innocence at your trial," he said.

I didn't know who these guards were, or who they were working for, but I was pretty sure they weren't arresting me on behalf of the emperor. My best guess was that a coup of some sort was under way, and I'd been caught supporting the wrong side. Just my luck.

"So I'm under arrest, is that it?" I said.

"Yes. You are to come with us. If you are innocent, you have nothing to fear. Only the guilty need fear the tribunal."

"The tribunal?"

"Your guilt or innocence will be determined by a military tribunal."

"I see." This was great news. Just what I needed - to have my guilt or innocence determined by some military tribunal that had taken over the country. "Exactly who's running the country these -" I started to say, but was cut off by the guard.

"Enough questions. I've already told you, you have nothing to worry about if you're truly innocent. Now it is time to go."

I nodded, as if to agree with him, but there was something about the way he told me all this that led me not to believe him. I got the impression if I got a trial - and that was a big if - I wouldn't really get the opportunity to demonstrate my innocence. Under these circumstances, there was only one reasonable thing for me to do, so I did it - I turned around and sprinted away, running as fast as I could.

I learned an interesting lesson from this course of action, and it goes like this - while a human can easily outrun a Podok, it it much more difficult to outrun a shot fired from a Podok's stungun. I hadn't gone more than a yard or two when the stunshot hit me and knocked me down.

Apparently the shot that hit me was of low power, because I was still conscious. Not only was I conscious, but all my body parts seemed to be working okay. As soon as I realized this, I scrambled to my feet and took off down the corridor, running as fast as my now slightly-uncoordinated legs would carry me.

Unfortunately for me, the second stunshot that hit me seemed to be of higher power than the first. Or perhaps it was a cumulative effect. Whichever, I felt my coordination leave me and then darkness started to close in. The last thing I remember seeing was the carpet in the corridor rushing toward my face.

Chapter 10

I woke up on the floor of a dungeon - a real, honest-to-goodness dungeon, with stone walls and floors and huge metal bars to keep me in. My head hurt big time. I rolled over and sat up, squeezing my head between my hands to keep it from exploding, and took a look around.

Yeah, that's what it was, all right. A dungeon. No mistake. I'd thought for a second the whole thing might be an unpleasant hallucination caused by my stunshot hangover, but it wasn't. It was real.

I staggered to my feet - again squeezing my head - and stumbled over to the metal-barred door. It was, as I'd expected it would be, securely locked. I shook it a couple of times to vent my frustration, but it was so solid and heavy it didn't even move. All that happened was my head hurt more.

Well, this was a fine mess I'd gotten myself into. I shouldn't have gone wandering around the palace without Raz. If he'd been with me, all this might have turned out a lot differently.

I wondered what had happened to Raz, anyway. For all I knew, he was still asleep in his room, completely unaware a coup - or whatever was going on - was happening around him. Just sacked out cold, dreaming dreams of ... of whatever it is Podoks dream about.

Yeah, right. That seemed highly unlikely. What was more probable was that Raz had also been arrested. And if he had been, he was probably here in the dungeon, like me. Maybe even in the cell next door.

"RAZ!" I called out. "Are you in here?" My voice cracked from dryness - I would have killed for a Moon Cola - and the sound of it made the top of my head feel as if it was going to melt.

I listened carefully but there was no answer, so I called again, as loudly as I could. Still there was no reply. It was then an ugly thought entered my mind - what if Raz had refused to be arrested? What if he'd resisted and been fatally stunned?

Nah. I was still alive, wasn't I? And if I was still alive, so was Raz. Probably.

Of course, our situations were a lot different, Raz's and mine. I was a human, visiting from a planet that, until now, had enjoyed a peaceful relationship with Tetepu and the rest of the planet Pode. If this were an attempt to topple the current government, the would-be new leaders might not want to risk antagonizing Earth by killing me. Raz, on the other hand, was just another Podok - at least, from their point of view - and had no such protection.

Far off in the distant recesses of the dungeon, the sound of footsteps on stone caught my attention and rescued me from the useless speculation in which I'd been engaged. I listened. They got louder.

I moved away from the door and toward the back of my cell - which wasn't far, since the cell was only about eight feet deep - and waited as the footsteps got louder and, obviously, closer. While I waited, I tried to figure out who was coming from the sounds of the footsteps. Here in this dungeon, with echoes bouncing off the stone walls, that was no easy task.

I decided there were three of them - Podoks, of course - and two of them were guards and the other one, the one in the middle, was a prisoner. Perhaps it was even Raz.

Or maybe not. The source of the footsteps turned out to be only one Podok, and it wasn't Raz. It was the Tetepuan Defense Minister, General Noz-ti Pem. Or Nasty Noz-ti, as Raz and I had taken to calling him.

"Hello, Mr. Denton," General Noz-ti said through the bars of my cell. "It's good to see you again, although it appears it could be under more favorable circumstances. You seem to have gotten yourself into a bit of legal difficulty."

"General Noz-ti," I said to him. "Now, why am I not surprised at seeing you here?"

He grinned broadly at me and said, "I'm afraid I have some bad news for you."

I braced myself, half-expecting the bad news to be about Raz, but it wasn't.

"I have the results from your trial," he said.

"Trial? What trial?"

"That would be your trial on charges of participating in the attempt on Emperor Fen's life."

"Why don't I remember this?" I said.

"Well, you were unable to attend, due to ... medical complications." The general flashed his teeth in a particularly unpleasant smile.

"Medical complications?"

"You were unconscious."

"I see. Let me guess - I was found guilty of all charges."

"Why, that's right," said General Noz-ti, feigning surprise. "That's quite a gift you have there - I didn't realize humans had psychic powers."

"So what happens next? Are you going to send me back to Earth?"

"Send you back to Earth? You'd like that, wouldn't you? No. No, indeed. We're going to execute you."

"Execute me?" I was sure I must have heard him wrong. Or maybe my vox-box had made a mistake - they aren't perfect.

"Yes, that's right. Execute. As in, put to death."

"You're kidding, right?"

The smile disappeared from Nasty Noz-ti's face and was replaced by the look that had helped earn him that nickname in the first place. "Kidding?" he said. "No kidding is involved, Mr. Denton. Tomorrow morning you will be executed, as ordered by the Tribunal. Only the fact it will take that long to prepare the execution chamber keeps you from being dead already." He tacked another nasty grin onto this statement and then turned and started to walk away.

Even though I knew it wasn't a good idea, I couldn't resist blurting out, "You're not going to slow roast me over an open flame, are you?"

General Noz-ti stopped and looked back at me, then gave a little, evil-sounding laugh. "My, that is an interesting idea," he said, "but, unfortunately, it would take too long and be much too noisy. You'll be executed by lethal injection. It's quick and painless - you should be thanking me."

"Thanks a lot!" I called after him as he walked away. I meant it to sound super-sarcastic, but the vox-box apparently missed the sarcasm, because Nasty Noz-ti called back, "Don't mention it," and waved his hand at me, as if I'd really thanked him.

I sat down on the floor - my cell had absolutely nothing in it except a foul-smelling hole in the floor - and tried to keep the tiny bit of panic lodged in the pit of my stomach from exploding into a full-blown anxiety attack.

This was certainly something I'd never thought about when I agreed to come back to Pode to make the flik - that I'd end up being sentenced to death. And, perhaps, being executed.

I say 'perhaps' because I could not quite believe what was happening to me. If what Noz-ti Pem had said was true - and I assumed it was - I had only a few hours to live. What I really needed now was a savior, a Podok who saves the lives of humans. Someone like Raz.

Raz. I could almost see him, standing there, a serious look on his face, saying, "This is not good." And I had to agree - this certainly was not good.

I wondered anew if he was here, somewhere in the dungeon. The place was gigantic and he could have been so far away he didn't hear me calling to him earlier. Or he might have been still unconscious, if they'd stunned him. I decided to try calling out again, and I did, but the results were the same as the first time - no answer.

I sat back down and resumed considering my bleak future. The possibility I might not be the only one to be executed in the morning occurred to me. There were all those human actors - including Donna -

out on Momasu Island, for example. A change of government could be just as dangerous for them as it had proved for me.

Of course, all my ruminations were based on the idea a coup was in progress, and that someone - Noz-ti Pem would be a good guess - was trying to take over the government. It was possible I was wrong about that, and something entirely different was going on. If so, I couldn't imagine what else it might be.

I leaned back against the stone wall and closed my eyes. Religion had never been a big part of my life, but I'd always believed in a higher power, and now I had a few personal words with Him. Or Her. Or It. I hesitate to call it praying - it was more like silent pleading for my life.

At some point during this one-sided conversation, I fell asleep for a few moments. Difficulty in staying awake seems to be a frequent after-effect of getting stunned, especially if you close your eyes for any length of time. Otherwise I'm sure that, given the fix I was in, I wouldn't have been able to sleep.

I awoke to the sounds of footsteps approaching my cell - surely it couldn't be time for my execution already? Panic began to spread through me and I looked around wildly for someplace - anyplace - to hide. There wasn't any.

"Roger?" came a voice from outside my cell. "Are you in here? Where are you?"

I stood up and looked through the bars. A single Podok - a female - was standing in the huge corridor that ran past my cell. It was Princess Sesu.

"Princess?" I said. "What are you doing here?"

"I've come to help you escape," she said. "We have to hurry. They're planning to execute you." She came over to my cell door and inserted a chipcard into the lock.

A rather strange combination, I thought - this ancient, metal-barred door being controlled by a modern, electronic lock, but the door sprung open nonetheless. "What's happening?" I said, as I slipped through the doorway and joined her in the corridor. "Is it a coup?"

"Yes." She grabbed me by the hand. "Come on. We have to leave."

"Where are your parents? And Prince Stee?"

"I don't know. General Noz-ti's men came and took them away. But I hid. Ooh, I hate that Podok. I'd like to -"

"Later," I said. "You can do all that later. Slow roast him, if you like. But first we've got to stop this coup. And that means we've got to find Raz. We'll need his help."

"He's here, in the dungeon, I'm sure. I just don't know exactly where."

"Well, then let's find him."

We wandered along the corridor, searching the cells on each side for Raz. Actually, calling it a corridor doesn't accurately describe the space between the cells on one side of the dungeon and those on the other side. The distance from one side to the other was easily 20 feet.

We found Raz locked in a cell at the far end of the dungeon, a long way from where I'd been imprisoned. Apparently they wanted to keep us apart. Or perhaps there were separate parts of the dungeon for Podoks and non-Podoks.

Whatever, he was leaning on his tail, looking perfectly calm, as if he knew it was just a matter of time until I came to rescue him. "Roger," he said, "I'm happy to see you. And Princess Sesu. It is good to see you both." Because of the presence of the princess, he spoke in Podok, and I heard the translation.

"Come on. We have to hurry," Princess Sesu said, unlocking Raz's cell. "They'll be coming for you soon."

Raz slipped through the open cell door and the three of us headed toward the exit, which was the same door as the entrance, and was located at the opposite end of the dungeon from where we were.

"How did you get in here, Roger?" Raz asked me as we hurried along. I use the word 'hurried,' but it really fails to convey the speed at which we moved. What a Podok calls hurrying, a human would call a casual stroll.

"Just like you," I said. "I was arrested - stunned, actually - and locked in a cell. Somewhere right about here, I think." I indicated the cells we were passing with a sweep of my hand. "Princess Sesu saved me, just like she saved you," I added.

"Thank you, Princess," Raz said. "I am more than appreciative."

"The princess who saves the lives of humans and Podoks," I chipped in, causing her to smile. "I also thank you."

We came to the end of the corridor. A ramp, six or seven feet wide, led up to the arch-shaped entrance/exit door, the bottom of which was at least as far above the corridor floor as the ramp was wide. We started up it.

It occurred to me at this point that this was the only way in and out of the dungeon, and Princess Sesu must also have entered through this door. "Princess," I said, "is this the way you came in?"

"Of course," she said. "It's the only way."

"Weren't there any guards outside?"

"Well, there was one."

"What happened to him?"

"I shot him with his own stungun. It was on his desk. He was so surprised to see me - I just walked right over, picked it up and shot him. He started to say something, and then he just sank to the floor. I left him there and went looking for you and Raz."

"What happened to the stungun?"

"I put it back on the desk."

"Let's hope that guard was the only one," Raz said. "But I'd be surprised if that were true. Especially since -" He looked up at the door.

Princess Sesu and I followed Raz's gaze to the end of the ramp, and what we saw there was not particularly reassuring. As we watched, the door opened and three big Podok guards - Nasty Noz-ti's men, without a doubt - came through it and headed down the ramp toward us. It looked like our escape plans had, for the time being, at least, been delayed.

Chapter 11

We backed slowly down the ramp as the three guards advanced on us. When we got to the floor, I grabbed Princess Sesu by the arm and steered her away from where I expected the fight to take place.

"What are you doing, Roger?" she said to me.

"You stay here, where you won't get hurt," I said.

"Oh, poo," she said. "That won't be any fun."

The three guards advanced on Raz's position, slowly surrounding him. They appeared to be unarmed - as guards usually are when they go into a dungeon or prison - and I took that as a good sign. The fact it was three against one I took as a bad sign, but not a *really* bad sign, if you know what I mean. I'd seen Raz in action and I knew he was more than capable of taking care of himself. After all, he was a professional bodyguard for the royal family.

"So, Raz, you've made your decision," one of the guards said. "You won't be joining us?"

"No," Raz said. "I am loyal to the current government."

"Too bad," said the guard, and as he said it, he stepped toward Raz and planted his big, elephant-like front foot solidly between them.

I'm pretty sure his intention was to execute a spinning tail slap, a basic but extremely deadly move from the Podok martial art of *mak su* - tail fighting. Although it looks easy enough - you pivot on your front foot, spin and snap your tail, like a whip, at your adversary - Raz, who's a mak su master, has told me it takes years of training to learn how to control an 80-pound tail moving at such a high speed. And if it lands - if you actually hit someone with that tail, well, too bad for them.

Fortunately for Raz and us and unfortunately for the guard, he never completed the move. He got to the point where you're supposed to pivot on your front foot, but as he started to turn, Raz was already well into his counter-move, which consisted of stepping forward and planting a stiff-legged kick into the side of his opponent's leg. The leg buckled in a way I'm sure it wasn't designed to do and the guard fell to the floor, screaming in pain.

"Aren't you going to help Raz?" Princess Sesu said to me.

"Help him? Does he look like he needs help? No, I'm not going to help him."

"Really?"

"Really. The thought never even entered my mind."

"Why not?"

"Well, first of all, Raz can take care of himself. You know that - you just saw an example."

"And second?"

"Second? Second is, I'm too smart to get involved. I'm a head shorter and 60 or 70 kilos lighter than any one of those guards, and I make it a point not to get into fights with those I know can beat the stuffing out of me."

"I suppose that's a good strategy."

"Good? It's excellent."

"But there's two of them and just Raz."

"Yeah. I feel sorry for them. They're hopelessly unqualified for this match."

So we stood there and watched as the two remaining guards circled cautiously around Raz, who stood nearly motionless between them. I say 'nearly motionless' because, although Raz's legs and arms and body and head remained perfectly still, his tail was twitching like an angry cat's. Off to the side, the third guard lay on the floor, holding his leg and moaning loudly. He wouldn't be returning to the fray anytime soon.

The action had slowed considerably since Raz's brief encounter with the first guard. After what had happened to him, the other two guards seemed reluctant to mix it up. In fact, Raz and the two guards had just about stopped moving, altogether. The three of them stood there, out of reach of one another, eyeing each other suspiciously and waiting for someone to make the first move.

It was Princess Sesu who finally made that move. "This is boring," she said, and before I could stop her, she took a couple of steps forward and kicked one of the guards - the one with his back to us - under his tail, up high where it joins his body.

The guard expelled the contents of his lungs with a loud whooshing sound and collapsed to the floor, apparently unconscious. The princess turned to me and flashed those big sharp teeth of hers in a smile. "Private parts," she said. "Very delicate."

This little distraction was all Raz needed. The remaining guard glanced briefly at his fallen comrade, and that turned out to be a major mistake on his part. Raz's tail came spinning around, aimed at the guard's head and traveling so fast it was a blur.

At the last instant the guard saw it coming and tried to duck, but it was too late. Raz's tail slammed into the top part of his head and snapped it sideways with a terrible crunching noise. The guard toppled to the floor without making a sound.

"Ouch," I said.

Raz grinned at me. "To be going," he said in English, and then in Podok, "Let's go."

The guards had conveniently left the door at the top of the ramp open for us. In the office, just on the other side of the door, we found the still-unconscious guard whom Princess Sesu had shot, and the stungun with which she'd shot him. I picked up the stungun and tucked it into the waistband of my jeans, leaving my T-shirt out to cover it.

"Come on, let's go," said Raz.

Princess Sesu led us along a hallway, through a door, down some steps to another hallway, along that to another door, and through that. When we went through the last door, we came out in a dirt-floored tunnel, one of many that passed beneath the palace. In long ago, more violent times, the tunnel system provided a last-chance means of escape if the palace came under an attack that couldn't be repelled.

The princess appeared to know where she was going as she led us through a series of interconnecting tunnels with scarcely a pause to consider our route. A year ago, on my first visit to Pode, she and I had become lost exploring these same tunnels, but now she seemed to be quite sure of her way through the confusing maze. I mentioned this to her.

"Oh, that," she said. "Well, after we got lost, I decided I'd better learn my way around before bringing any more guests down here."

"I see."

"Or, who knows? Maybe we weren't really lost at all that time. Maybe I just faked the whole thing, so we could be alone together." She flashed me a wicked grin.

I didn't know what to believe. She'd had a crush on me back then, and it was entirely conceivable she'd gotten us lost on purpose. In fact, I'd thought so at the time, but she'd denied it.

Whatever. It didn't really matter. That was then and this was now. All that mattered was that she knew her way out of the tunnels now.

And she did. After what seemed like miles of walking, we emerged into the cool night air.

"Where are we?" said Raz.

"North of the palace," said Princess Sesu. "On the other side of Opiza Hill."

The location meant nothing to me. Without someone to guide me, I couldn't find my way from one end of the palace to the other. Areas of Tapu were totally beyond my comprehension. "So. What's the plan?" I said.

"Plan?" said the princess.

"Plan?" said Raz.

"Yeah, plan. You know, like, what do we do next?"

"That's a very good question, Roger," the princess said. "I don't know, really. My plan was to save you and Raz, and I've done that."

"Well, we can't stop now," I said. "We have to rescue your parents and stop this coup before it's too late."

"I have an idea," Raz said.

Both the princess and I turned to him expectantly. "What?" she said.

"We need a place to hide out and we need someone - someone we can trust - to help us. How about your friend, Slar? He would seem to be a good candidate."

"Yes, Slar would be excellent," agreed Princess Sesu. "Don't you think so, Roger?"

"I trust him," I said.

"Good," said the princess. "Let's find a public vidcom and call him."

The tunnel had exited on the back side of Opiza Hill, a couple of hundred yards above the surrounding landscape. We hiked across the hill until we came to a street, then followed that down the hill. We ended up in a commercial district called, not surprisingly, Opiza, but since it was still the middle of the night, everything was closed.

We followed the pedestrian pathway that ran alongside the street until we came to a bank of vidcoms, all the while keeping watch for any military vehicles that might be out searching for us. Fortunately, there was no traffic of any kind, so looking out for General Noz-ti's men wasn't much of a problem.

"You call him, Princess," I said. "Tell him what's going on and ask him if he'll help us." I was sure Slar wouldn't turn down a request from the princess.

"All right. I need a chipcard."

I reached in my pockets and found them empty - my chipcard was gone. Across from me, Raz was having the same experience. I looked at him and he looked at me and then we both looked at Princess Sesu. "Don't you have one?" I said to her.

"No," she said. "I've never needed one before."

"Don't worry," Raz said. "We can charge the call to Slar. I'm sure he'll accept it."

"Sure," I said. "But you know what? A lot more than just our chipcards are missing. Nasty Noz-ti has our Imperial Passes, too."

"He'll probably try to use them as proof the emperor wants him to run the country," Raz said.

"I wouldn't be surprised," I said.

"Call Slar, Princess," said Raz.

"Yeah. And when he asks who's calling, identify yourself as Sesu, not Princess Sesu, just in case anyone's listening."

"What if he doesn't know who I am? Lots of Podok women are named Sesu."

"Then tell him it's Sesu from the Valley. From last summer. Be creative."

The princess managed, without much difficulty, to get us connected to Slar's. The com rang for what seemed like several minutes, and then I heard a sleepy-sounding voice agreeing to take our call. A couple of seconds later, an equally sleepy-looking face filled up the screen.

"Slar, this is Sesu," said the princess. "I'm in trouble. I'm with Raz and our friend from last summer, and we need your help."

"What's wrong?"

"I don't want to say right now - I'll tell you later. Do you have transportation?"

"I have a car."

"Will you pick us up?"

"Of course, Princess."

"Don't call me that. I'm just Sesu."

"Oh. Of course. I understand. Exactly where are you? I'll come get you."

Princess Sesu told him our location and disconnected. "It'll be a while," she said. "He lives on the other side of Tapu."

The three of us stood there, waiting pretty much in silence, for several minutes. The night air was warm and slightly moist, and smelled faintly of sweet flowers. It was all very reminiscent of Hawaii. I let my thoughts wander.

Finally, after several minutes minutes of silence, Raz said, "We still need a plan."

"What?" I said. In my mind, Donna and I were lying on a white sand beach, under a warm Hawaiian sun, drinking mai tais.

"A plan," Raz said.

"Yes," said Princess Sesu, just back from her own thoughts. "Once we get to Slar's house, then what? We'll be safe, I guess, but my parents and Stee will still be missing, and we won't be any closer to finding them than we are now."

"Don't worry about that," I said. "The first thing is to make sure you're safe, Princess. Once we accomplish that, I have a plan for Raz and me."

"You don't want me to help you?" she said. "Why not? I can take care of myself. If it wasn't for me, you and Raz would still be in the dungeon. Or worse."

"I know, Princess, and I appreciate all you've done for both of us. But now it's time to step aside and let us handle things."

"Why? Because you're males?"

"No, that's not it at all. It's because you're a princess, a member of the royal family."

"So what?"

"Well, I hadn't wanted to mention this because I didn't want to upset you, but consider this. You might be the last of the Da-mo family. You might be the last legitimate contender for the crown."

"Me? Don't be silly. Only males can rule, and Stee -" All at once she realized what I was hinting at, and she stopped talking and just stared at me.

"Are you all right, Sesu?" I said.

"You mean they might be dead? All of them?" she said.

"They might be. It's something we have to consider, at least. Don't you think so, Raz?"

"Yes, I'm afraid it's true. They could be already dead."

"Oh, no," Princess Sesu said. "This can't be happening."

"I'm sorry," I said, "but you can see why we have to keep you safe, just in case. Maybe they aren't dead. Let's hope so. Maybe Noz-ti's men have just stashed them somewhere, waiting until they see how all this turns out."

"Oh, do you think so?"

"It's possible. And if they are still alive, Raz and I will find them and rescue them." I wasn't sure exactly how Raz and I were going to do that, but just hearing my words in the open air made me feel better, and I'm pretty sure it had a cheering effect on Princess Sesu, too. "Won't we, Raz?" I added.

"Yes, if they are still alive, we will rescue them," Raz said. He said it with such conviction there was no doubting him.

The sound of a vehicle approaching cut through our conversation. The three of us moved away from the bank of vidcoms and into the shadows of a nearby building, just in case it turned out to be some of General Noz-ti's men, out looking for us. Unfortunately, because of the rather deliberate speed at which Podoks move, we didn't quite make it to the darkness of the shadows without being seen.

A Podok policeman, standing on one of those noisy flying platforms the local police use, swooped in on us and stopped about 15 feet away. "Halt!" he called to us.

We stopped and turned around.

"What are you doing out here?" he said.

Raz stepped forward to answer the question. "We made a call on the vidcom," he said. "To a friend. To come pick us up. Now we're just waiting for him to show up."

"Why did you run away when I approached?" said the cop, who was a local Tapu patrol officer, not a member of the PNP.

Princess Sesu stepped forward to handle this one. "That was my idea," she said. "When we heard you coming, we thought it was our friend, so we were going to hide and then jump out and scare him. Silly, huh?"

"Yes, it is," agreed the officer. "Who's the human?"

My turn. I stepped forward and said, in as dramatic a voice as I could manage, "Rocket Bomms, actor extraordinaire, at your service," I said. And then I bowed.

"You're that Roger Denton fellow," said the cop. "The human who saves the lives of Podoks. Right?"

I laughed. "Would that I were, kind sir. Would that I were. Alas, I am but portraying the courageous Mr. Denton in a lavish, multi-billion credit production of -"

"Okay, okay, I get it," said the officer. "You're not the real Roger Denton."

"Unfortunately, no." I let my head hang slightly. All in all, I thought it was a great performance. I would have made a great Roger Denton, if this palace intrigue stuff hadn't cut short my flik career.

"Don't you folks know about the curfew?" said the cop.

"Curfew?" said Raz.

"What curfew?" said Princess Sesu.

"Where have you three been?" said the cop. "Haven't you seen the news?"

"No," said Raz. "What's going on?"

"There was another attempt on Emperor Fen's life earlier today. It failed, but the emperor and his family are temporarily in hiding, and General Noz-ti Pem is running the country."

"I see," Raz said. "So that's why there's a curfew?"

"Yes."

"Are we under arrest?" said Princess Sesu.

"No. The police aren't enforcing the curfew - the military's in charge. We're just warning those we see to get off the streets. If the military catches you out here, though, you will be arrested."

"Well, thank you for the information, officer," Raz said. "We'll stay out of sight until our friend arrives to pick us up, and then we'll get off the streets as soon as we can."

"See that you do," said the cop. He banked his platform toward us and took off down the street.

We watched him until he rounded a corner and disappeared from our sight. I looked at Raz and Princess Sesu. They looked at me and at each other. Suddenly all three of us started to giggle.

Chapter 12

"Rocket Bomms?" said Princess Sesu. "You're an actor named Rocket Bomms?" Both she and Raz howled with laughter.

"Would that I were the famous Roger Denton, kind sir," said Raz with a mock bow, and the howls became shrieks.

"Hey, I didn't make that up, you know," I said. "That's the name of the actor who's playing me in the flik. Rocket Bomms." I was having a tough time controlling my own laughter.

While we were busy releasing our pent-up nervousness, Slar arrived in his quiet little electric car. We never heard him coming. "What's going on?" he said. "I thought this was an emergency."

"It is, it is," said Princess Sesu between giggles. "We have to get out of here before -"

The sound of another vehicle - a loud, noisy vehicle - interrupted her and drew our attention to the the end of the street. Rounding the corner and heading toward us was a large blue and gold military vehicle.

"Troops!" said Raz. "Come on, we have to get out of here."

The three of us piled into Slar's little electric sedan, the designers of which evidently never considered the possibility someone larger than a small Podok child might occupy the back seat. Slar kept apologizing for the lack of interior room and we kept telling him to forget about it, but someone really ought to send those designers a note. Anyway, with some difficulty the three of us managed to get in the car and get the door shut.

"Let's go! Let's go!" Princess Sesu shouted as the large military vehicle - Raz said it was a troop carrier - rumbled toward us.

Slar pushed man-op, slipped the little car into gear and floored it. Actually, that's not true - that's just an expression I've always wanted to use. What Slar really did was push a couple of buttons and say something to the car, causing us to start moving forward. Everything in a Podok car, except the steering and brakes when set to manual, is controlled by buttons or voice commands.

"Come on! Hurry!" said the princess. "That thing is heading straight for us!"

I leaned across the princess and around Raz to look out the back window. Princess Sesu was right - the troop carrier was only a couple of hundred yards away and rumbling straight toward us. "I agree with Princess Sesu," I said. "We should hurry."

"I'm sorry," said Slar. "It's this car of mine - it has no power, no acceleration."

"That's the truth," said Raz. "This isn't much of a car."

"Well, you know, it's just Nami and me. We don't need a big, powerful car - or, at least, we never did until now. And we can't afford one, either. So this is what you get." Slar sounded both apologetic and a little angry. I suppose it's just like on Earth - insult a man's car and you insult the man. Or, in this case, the Podok.

"Don't worry about it, Slar," I said. "The car is fine. Just get us out of here as fast as you can."

The troop carrier - or, rather, someone inside it - was calling to us over a loudspeaker. I couldn't understand everything that was being said - the sound quality was so poor my vox-box couldn't translate most of it - but I did hear the word 'stop' several times, and once I heard the phrase 'shoot to kill.' I guess I could have asked one of my companions for a more complete translation, but it didn't really seem necessary - I understood enough to know what was going on.

"Hurry, hurry, hurry," chanted the princess. "They're going to shoot us."

Through the window I could see the carrier, now only 150-or-so yards away, had lowered a laser cannon into firing position. And it was aimed right at us. "Yeah, hurrying sounds like a good idea," I said.

Slar's little car slowly gained speed, but the carrier continued to close the distance between us. The first cross street was still about two blocks ahead of us. If we could make it around that corner before they blew us away, and maintain what little bit of speed we'd managed to attain, we'd be - at least, temporarily- blocked from the troop carrier's sight by a large building on the corner and we might - just might - get away. I mentally crossed my fingers.

A loud THUD sounded from troop carrier, and almost immediately a hole opened in the roadway right behind us. It suddenly occurred to me just how serious all this actually was. These guys - the ones chasing us, I mean - weren't fooling around.

Another loud THUD and a second hole opened off to our right. They were zeroing in on us, getting our range. One or two more shots and they'd have us. And we still were a long city block away from the corner and the relative safety of that big building.

"Come on, sweetie, you can do it. I know you can," said Slar, talking to his car.

The carrier was still gaining on us, but not as fast as it had been. That seemed, to me at least, to be a good sign. I started to mention this to the others, but before I could, a BOOM - which is what a THUD sounds like when it gets closer to you - signaled another shot. I decided not to say anything.

This last shot hit about 20 yards in front of us, off to our left, blowing a crater in the roadway, just like the other shots had done. The difference was this time the hole that opened up in the street was right in front of us, and it was huge. Slar yanked the little car to the right and then, just as quickly, back to the left, as he deftly maneuvered us around the crater. It was a nice piece of driving, but it sent me, Raz, and Princess Sesu sprawling.

"Sorry, guys," Slar said. "You, too, Princess."

"Don't worry about it," said the princess, clambering back to an upright position. "If you get us out of here, I'll forgive you."

"Not much farther," I said. "We might just make it."

Slar started to position his car to the left side of the road, setting up to take the tightest possible line through the upcoming turn to the right, without losing speed. As he moved the little car over, another BOOM sounded from behind us and a hole opened exactly parallel to us, in the location we'd just vacated. All four of us flinched and ducked away from the explosion, and only the fact we were still moving forward kept us from being hit by flying debris from the roadway.

"That was *too* close!" Princess Sesu said, and, although nobody else said anything, I was pretty sure we all agreed with her.

"Hang on," said Slar. "Here we go, around the corner."

I looked back at the troop carrier, which seemed to have lost some ground on us. We were almost around the corner, and we were maintaining our speed, which meant once we straightened out, we'd be able to run away from the carrier with ease. Our pursuers had lost their advantage - the race was over and we'd won.

Out of frustration perhaps, the carrier launched one more shot at us. The BOOM was once again a THUD, which confirmed my suspicion it was losing ground, and the shot hit harmlessly in the roadway behind us as we sped away. We were on a long, straight stretch of road now, and we continued to accelerate. Soon the troop carrier, which had followed us around the corner, disappeared into the night air behind us.

"All right," said Slar. "We made it."

"Nice driving, Slar," I said.

"I knew you could do it," said Princess Sesu.

"This little car is all right," said Raz.

Slar beamed. At least, he started to. But mid-beam, long before attaining maximum luminescence, his face froze. "Oh, oh," he said.

"What's wrong?" I said.

"Look!" Slar uncoiled one of his fingers and pointed upward, through the windshield.

I leaned forward and looked to see what had interrupted his beaming. Directly above us, at a height of only 200 feet or so, a big, dark, round shape was shadowing us. "A skimmer?" I said to Slar.

"A military skimmer. And they're right on top of us. What should I do?"

"Go in there," Raz said, indicating a three-story, roofed parking lot coming up on our left.

Slar slowed and turned into the lot, which was one of many surrounding a shopping center called Podok Paradise, or Podok Heaven - something to that effect. I never did get the name straight, but I guess it doesn't matter, since both names really mean the same thing.

"Now what?" Slar said, as we coasted to a stop in the nearly-empty parking lot.

"Maybe they don't know it's us," Raz suggested.

"You think?" said Princess Sesu.

"Yeah," I chipped in. "Maybe they were just following us because we were violating the curfew."

"So what do we do?" Slar said.

"See those cars over there?" Raz said. "They must belong to employees who either have to work late or come in early."

Since it was still somewhere between the middle of the night and early morning, and the shopping center was closed, Raz's theory made a lot of sense. I said as much.

"So let's move the car over there with the others, and if someone comes in to check, it'll just look like we were employees who didn't hear about the curfew, coming to work."

"What about us?" Princess Sesu said. "Where will we go?"

"We'll stay in the car," Raz said. "Slar, park us in the middle of a bunch of cars, if you can."

Slar moved the car across the parking lot and parked it with the other cars in what was apparently an employee parking section, carefully maneuvering us into a spot where we were surrounded on three sides by other cars, but still had a way to get out in a hurry, if we had to. All the other cars in the lot looked pretty much just like Slar's - tall, white igloos on four wheels - and I considered this to be a point in our favor. Maybe, if someone came to check, they wouldn't be able to pick this car out from the rest.

"What'll we do if someone comes?" Slar said.

"Just duck down," said the princess.

"You're kidding, right?" I said. "We just barely fit in here as it is, and you think we've got room to duck?"

"We're about to find out," Princess Sesu said. "Look what's coming."

Raz, Slar and I followed her gaze. Coming across the parking lot at a very slow speed, with only inches of clearance both beneath it and above it, was the military skimmer.

"They're crazy, coming in here with a skimmer," Raz said. "There's not enough room."

"They must know it's us," I said.

"Yeah, maybe they do."

We tried to duck down and hide, but it was no use. For one thing, there wasn't enough room. And for another, the military skimmer stopped right next to us and announced that if we didn't surrender, our car - and us, too, presumably - would be vaporized.

Faced with spending our remaining days as vapors, we did what any intelligent humans or Podoks would do. We surrendered. But just as we were about to get out of Slar's car, an idea came to me.

"Raz, you were in the military. Right?"

"Yes."

"How many Podoks are in that skimmer, do you think?"

"Probably just two, a driver and a guard."

"You think that's all?"

"There could be more. But two would be normal."

"So let's take them out." I briefly outlined my plan.

First, Slar got out of the car. He stood there facing the skimmer with his arms sticking straight up and his hands clasping each other, which I assume was the proper way to surrender to authorities on Pode. Or, at least, in Tetepu.

Then Princess Sesu got out and stood very close to Slar, on his right. She, too, put her arms straight up and clasped her hands together.

Raz was next, taking a position on Slar's left and also very close to him. He, too, went through the arms up, hands together routine.

Finally, it was my turn. I exited the vehicle and found myself - as we'd planned all along - hidden behind an almost-solid Podok wall consisting of my three friends. Slowly, the four of us - me holding my stungun tightly in my hand - moved toward the skimmer.

When we were 10 or 12 feet away, the skimmer door slid open, revealing two Podoks clad in the drab blue uniforms of the Tetepuan Defense Force. One was at the controls and the other stood in the doorway, casually brandishing a stungun and looking pretty pleased with himself.

"Thought you could escape, did you?" he said, stepping down from the skimmer onto the pavement and taking a step toward us.

"How foolish of us," said Raz.

"Yes, it was," said the soldier. Suddenly, he seemed to realize I was missing, and a look of alarm came over his face. "What happened to the human?" he said sharply.

"What human?" said Slar.

"You know what human - the one who was in the car with you."

"That would be me," I said, and as I said it, I leaned around my Podok 'wall' and shot him. Twice. I tried to shoot the driver, too, but he was too quick for me. Before I could get him in my sights, the skimmer lurched forward.

That could have been bad news for us - he could have escaped and called for reinforcements, for example - but we were lucky. As the skimmer jumped forward, trying to escape, it slammed right into several of the many cars parked around us. The skimmer pilot, who'd been unprepared for such a sudden stop, was sent flying head-first into the windshield, rendering him unconscious. Judging by the way the pilot looked – 'smashed' is the word I'd use to describe him - the anti-gravity system had failed to function properly. I think that had something to do with the door being open. The skimmer also suffered significant damage.

That meant a slight change in our plan, which had been to steal the skimmer. Instead, we piled back into Slar's tiny car and headed out of the parking lot, onto the highway. As we slowly accelerated up to cruising speed, we were in good spirits, laughing and joking and bragging about how we'd taken out that military skimmer, and exuding confidence in our plans both to turn back the coup and to find Princess Sesu's family alive. Still, deep inside, I knew this was the 'Podok curse' at work, and I couldn't help but worry about what lay ahead of us.

Chapter 13

It was just starting to get light when we got to Slar's. The neighborhood residents all still seemed to be sleeping - houses were dark and, with the exception of a faint whistling sound caused by a rather brisk wind, the area was silent. We got out of the car and into the house as quickly and as quietly as possible, not wanting to alert the neighbors of our arrival. As Raz said, you never can be sure where loyalties lie.

Nami, Slar's wife, helped us into the kitchen and positioned us around a large, oval table there, finding a box for me to sit on. "I was really worried," she said as she served steaming hot cups of some mysterious black Podok beverage to us. "I expected you back long ago - I thought you got arrested."

"We almost did," Slar said.

"But your husband's terrific driving ability saved us," I said.

Nami smiled. "Well, he is a professional driver," she said.

I took a tentative sip of my drink. It tasted suspiciously like coffee. Real coffee, not the imitation Pode kind. "Nami, is this real coffee?" I said.

"Yes, it is. It's imported - one of the little luxuries we allow ourselves. But they've started growing it here on Pode now, too, you know."

I hadn't known, but I wasn't surprised. Podoks had already adopted so many aspects of Earth culture that I wasn't a bit surprised to find drinking coffee among them. They had pizza and fried chicken and plantburgers and soft drinks. Why not coffee? "It's good," I said.

"Are you folks hungry?" Nami said. "I could make some breakfast."

The four of us - Princess Sesu, Raz, Slar and myself - looked at each other and then at Nami and then back at each other again. "I don't know about anybody else," I said, "but I'm starved."

The other three quickly agreed with me, so Nami set about preparing some food to go with the excellent-tasting coffee. While she did that, the rest of us tried to come up with a plan of attack.

"I think we have to go back to the palace," I said.

"What for?" said Princess Sesu. "To get arrested again?"

"No, that wasn't what I had in mind. But we have to find out what happened to your family, and the palace is the place to get that information."

"Yes," said Raz. "Someone at the palace must know what happened. And not everyone who works there is involved in this coup attempt. In fact, I'm sure the great majority of palace employees are loyal to the emperor. And very few are fond of General Noz-ti."

"All except the guards," I noted.

"But you'll be arrested on sight," said Princess Sesu. "Or worse."

"That is a problem," I agreed.

"You should go during the news conference," said Nami from her stove, where she was preparing something my vox-box translated as 'breakfast stew.'

"What news conference?" I said.

"Oh, I was watching news while I was waiting for you. They said General Noz-ti had called a news conference for mid-day. He's going to tell the nation what's really going on."

"I'll just bet," said Princess Sesu with a touch of anger.

"I can see it now," I said.

"Me, too," said Raz. "He's going to say the emperor has asked him to take over - temporarily, of course - and then he'll show our Imperial Passes as proof."

"There must be something we can do to stop him," Princess Sesu said.

"Maybe there is," I said. "Nami, do you know where this news conference is going to be held?"

"In front of the palace, on the big steps."

"Really? That's perfect. While everyone is busy out front, we'll sneak in the back way. What do you think, Raz?"

"Maybe. Maybe we could do that."

"That's good," said Princess Sesu. "And I've thought of something I can do to help, too."

"Now, Princess -" I said, starting to give her the speech about keeping her safe in case she was the last of the Da-mo family.

She cut me off. "I know, I know. You want me to stay out of it. But this is a good idea. A *really* good idea."

I knew arguing with her was useless - after all, she was a princess and used to getting her own way - so I shrugged and said, "What is it?"

"I have lots of friends among the media," she said. "What if I got in touch with some of them and went to General Noz-ti's news conference with them - disguised as a reporter or a camera operator or something, I mean. Then, when he says all these things, I can rise up and denounce him as a liar who's trying to take over the government by force."

"Hmm, that is a good idea. What do you think, Raz?"

"I agree," he said. "It's a good plan."

The princess smiled. "And if you two sneak in the back at the same time, my confrontation with Noz-ti will act as a diversion."

"Sounds good to me," I said. "Excellent, actually."

"Me, too," said Raz.

"What about me?" said Slar.

"I'm sorry, Slar," I said. "We appreciate the help you've given us so far, but there's no room for you in the rest of the plan. You'll stay here with Nami."

"But -"

"That's right," said Princess Sesu. "Slar, your job is to stay here and take care of your wife. I order it."

That pretty much put an end to that discussion. Slar looked disappointed, but Nami's face showed only relief. She set about serving us bowls of 'breakfast stew' with a big, happy grin on her face.

"You know, Slar," said Princess Sesu, "there is one thing you can do for me, though."

"Anything, Princess. Anything at all."

"Once we've finished eating and it's fully light out and the curfew's no longer in effect, you can drive me down to the Central News building."

"What are we going to do there?"

"*We're* not going to do anything. You're going to drop me off, then turn around and come right back here and take care of Nami, like I said."

"Oh," was all Slar had to say to that.

After breakfast, we firmed up our plans, making sure the three of us each knew what to do and when to do it, then Princess Sesu and Slar left for the Central News building, downtown. The princess thought she could get help from several reporters and recordists she knew there, and I was sure she was right. Princess Sesu was immensely popular with the media - more so, by far, than any other member of the royal family - and even I knew a couple of local media types who would have done just about anything for her.

After Slar and the princess left, Raz and I still had a lot of time to kill until the news conference. Nami solved that minor problem for us by offering to let us use the giant - by human standards - bed in her and Slar's bedroom. It had been a while since either Raz or I had had any natural sleep, and it might be longer still until our next chance, so we grabbed it. If I thought the coffee and the ongoing excitement might keep me awake, I was wrong - sleep swept over me within seconds of lying down.

I had an interesting dream. In it, I was one of a group of circus clowns. Raz, Princess Sesu, Slar and Nami were part of my clown group, as well as some others whose identities remained a mystery to me. We all had big red noses and huge floppy shoes and fright wigs - standard clown getup.

Anyway, in the dream, a tall, Earth-style building was on fire, and standing on top of the building, screaming for help, was my girlfriend, Donna. "Help me, Roger. Help me," she yelled.

My clown friends and I were in a tiny little car, and you had to pedal it to make it go - that was my job. It was tough because I had about a dozen Podok clowns jammed into the car with me, all of them honking their horns and acting goofy. I was pedaling as hard as I could, but we were barely making any progress at all.

Just as we were about to arrive at the fire, a flying tank, commanded by General Noz-ti, himself, showed up and began shooting at us. Raz, Princess Sesu, Slar, and Nami were all yelling at me to pedal faster, but I just didn't have the strength, so I stopped pedaling and started to get out of the car. The other clowns didn't seem to think getting out of the car was such a good idea - they were grabbing me and holding me but I made it, anyway.

Once I was out of the car, I could see Donna up on top of the burning building, but she was no longer yelling for help. Someone - a human - was on top of the building with her. He was wearing a superhero costume, with a long, flowing cape and a mask, and as I watched, he scooped Donna up in his arms and leaped off the building.

Over by the burning building, but on the ground, I saw another figure, partially hidden by shadows. I squinted, and at the same time, the figure stepped out into the light. It was my ex-wife, Linda, and she was shouting something at me. I yelled back at her, "What?" and she said, "I set the fire," and then she laughed that annoying laugh of hers as several Podok clowns pulled me back into the car.

I woke up. Slar was shaking me, telling me it was almost time to leave. I felt horrible - instead of feeling rested from my nap, I was exhausted. It must have been all that pedaling.

I sat up. Raz was just waking up on the other side of the bed. "Good morning," I said to him.

"Yes," he said, without a lot of enthusiasm. He looked like the way I felt. Maybe he'd had his own dream, or perhaps he just wasn't a morning Podok.

We freshened up in the bathroom and then gathered in the kitchen for more coffee before leaving. Nami was her usual chipper self, bouncing around the table, serving us. I wondered if she'd had a nap, too.

"What happened at the news building?" I asked Slar.

"I don't know. She made me drop her off outside and then drive away. The last I saw of her, she was standing there, waving at me."

"Can she prove who she is?" I said.

"I'm sure she can," Raz said. "Besides, she really does know several big shot media types - reporters, especially. She tips them off about things happening at the palace. Not political things, but gossip and personal trivia about the royal family and the rest of high society - who's mad at whom, who shouldn't be invited to the same party as someone else, that sort of thing."

"You all should relax," was Nami's unsolicited advice. "Princess Sesu can handle this with no problems - I'm sure of it. She's a lot tougher than you think."

"Yeah, I'm with Nami," I said. "The princess won't have any trouble."

We moved on to other topics of discussion - namely, our own plans.

"I'll drop you off, just like I did the princess," was Slar's offer.

"No, Slar. Taking the princess downtown was one thing, but there's no need for you to go near the palace," I said. "That place will be crawling with guards, and if you get caught with us, you'll be in big trouble."

"Really big trouble," agreed Raz.

"So how are you going to get there?" said Slar.

Raz grinned. "We're borrowing your car," he said.

"Oh," was Slar's only reaction, while Nami's was a smile. I'm sure, after only recently getting her husband back, she wasn't eager to lose him again, and was perfectly content to have him stay behind.

And that's the way it happened. When the time came, Raz and I finished our coffee, said goodbye to Slar and Nami, and drove away in their car.

The highway into Tapu was practically empty, even though it was a normal work day for most Podoks. Probably many residents were staying home, waiting for the mid-day announcement from General Noz-ti before venturing out. I mean, everyone knew something was going on - a dusk-to-dawn curfew for the entire country was not a normal occurrence in Tetepu.

We parked in a lot about two blocks from the palace, on the back side, away from where the news conference was just about ready to begin, if we'd timed things right. I'd told Slar this area would be heavily guarded, and I'd believed it when I said it, but so far we hadn't encountered any guards or soldiers at all. In fact, as Raz and I walked along the narrow road that led to the entrance for palace employees, we were the only signs of life.

"No one is on the street being," said Raz, who'd gone back to speaking English now that he and I were alone. "To be spooking."

"Spooky," I said. "Not spooking, spooky. And I agree. It is spooky."

"Roger, you are thinking something wrong is being?"

"I hope not. Maybe everyone is just at the news conference. Or inside, watching it on the wall."

"Yes. To be hoping."

We walked all the way up to the employee's entrance without encountering anyone. No vehicles drove by, either. It did seem more than a little strange.

To get into the palace this way, you had to go through the Employee's Entertainment Center, a long, three-story-high building that featured a bar and a restaurant, game rooms, computer rooms, a gymnasium and spa, and lots of other fun things, all for the use of palace employees and government officials. You also had to punch in, using your official government-issued I.D., at a desk which was manned at all times by an armed guard. I wondered aloud how we were going to get by this checkpoint.

"Not to worry, Roger," Raz said. "I am a plan for to be having."

"Good," I said, and let it go at that as I followed him into the building, being careful to stay far enough behind to avoid his tail, which was bouncing around nervously, as if it had a life of its own.

We met no one until we got to the desk, where the guard was leaning on his tail, watching the just-beginning news conference on a portable video screen and munching on some kind of chips. Raz's 'plan' turned out to be about what I'd expected - he walked right up to the desk, and when the guard looked up, Raz punched him in the throat. The guard - who didn't even have time to look surprised - went down in a heap, spilling his chips.

"I have a stungun, you know," I told Raz.

"Not to be needing." He grinned at me and picked up the fallen guard's stungun. "Now I too am having," he said.

"Great. We'll probably need them."

We made it all the way through the EEC and into the palace itself before we bumped into anyone else. Fortunately for us, that anyone was someone we both knew - Ten-zo Kiki, the young female Podok who had served me chili dogs on my first night staying at the palace. She seemed surprised to see Raz and me.

"Mr. Denton! Mr. An-zo! What are you doing here?"

"Why wouldn't we be here, Kiki?"

"But I thought -" She stopped.

"What?" said Raz, speaking Podok again.

"I thought you two were guarding Emperor Fen and his family."

"As you can see, we're not. In fact, we don't even know where they are, and we're trying to find out. Do you know?"

"No. What's going on?"

"We think it's a coup attempt," I said. "We think General Noz-ti is trying to take over the government."

"Oh, no," said Kiki. "That can't be. The emperor put General Noz-ti in charge. He has an Imperial Pass."

"That's what he wants everyone to believe. He has two I.P.s, but he stole them from me and Raz."

"Yes," said Raz. "So if you know anything ..."

"But I don't," said Kiki. "All I know is Emperor Fen, Empress Nememe, and Prince Stee all left, along with some armed guards. No one seems to know what happened to Princess Sesu."

"How did they leave?" I said.

"I think they took the big skimmer."

"By skimmer, huh?"

"Yes."

I patted Kiki on the arm and thanked her, then turned to Raz. "Come on, let's go check out the skimmer garage and see what we can find out."

"Yes," Raz said in English. "This is good. To be going." He turned and headed for the skimmer garage, and I fell in beside him.

Chapter 14

The skimmer garage - actually, it was more of a parking lot than a garage, with only a small portion of it having a roof - was deserted, as had been the palace hallways leading to it. Apparently most everyone in the palace was out front, listening to General Noz-ti tell his lies to the population of Tetepu. I wondered if Princess Sesu was in place, and how that was going.

"No one here is being for to be questioned," said Raz. "This is not good."

"It doesn't matter," I told him.

"No?"

"No. Kiki said they left in the big skimmer, right? Well, it's back, sitting right there. Why don't we just ask it where it's been?"

"Oh, this idea is good being."

I thought so, too. We crossed to the big skimmer and climbed in, closing the gull-wing doors behind us. Raz sat in the pilot's seat, and I sat on the edge of the seat next to him, being careful to remember not to slide back and fall into the tail tube.

"Skimmer, I need some information," said Raz. He was speaking Podok again.

"How may I assist you?" said the female voice of the skimmer's computer.

"Where did you go on your last trip?"

"I'm sorry, but that information has been classified and is restricted to those with level five clearance. Do you have such clearance?"

"No," Raz said. "Never mind."

"Maybe we can figure it out another way," I said.

"How?"

"Skimmer," I said, "we don't really need to know where you went. We just need to know the distance traveled, so we can ... uh, ... update our maintenance records."

"All such records are maintained in memory," said the skimmer. "Updating is automatic."

"Oh. Well, ..." I was still trying to think of another lie when the skimmer volunteered some information that made lying unnecessary.

"Distance and time logs are available without restriction," said the skimmer.

"Really?" I said. "How careless of General Noz-ti's troops not to restrict that, too."

The skimmer had no comment on this. It probably didn't even know what I was talking about.

"So, what was the distance recorded on your last trip?" I said.

"One thousand, one hundred and ninety-one kilometers," answered the skimmer.

"How is that figured, exactly? Is the distance recorded from each time you start up? Or what?"

"Distance is recorded continuously with each departure from home station."

"Home station? You mean, here?"

"Yes."

"I see. So it's a round-trip record, recorded from the time you leave here until you return. Right?"

"Yes. That is correct."

"I know where Emperor Fen and his family are, Raz," I said.

"Where?"

"At the country house, the same place the Mo-zens took Princess Sesu and me, last year. It's the perfect place to stash someone - it's only accessible by skimmer. You drop them off and they're stuck there - you don't even have to guard them. There's no way to escape."

"You and Princess Sesu were escaped," Raz reminded me.

"That was a fluke. It's not likely to happen again."

"Roger, you are sure this is where Emperor Fen is being?"

"Well, not 100 percent, no. But it fits. That's just about the right distance, and it would be a great spot to hide them. I have a hunch - a strong hunch - that's where they are. Besides, what else do we have to go on?"

"Uh, oh," said Raz.

"What?"

"Someone is coming."

I looked up to see two guards about 50 yards away, stunguns in hands, heading straight for our skimmer. Since the doors were closed and it's impossible to see through the one-way glass from the outside, I could only assume we'd set off a silent alarm when we entered. "Come on, let's get out of here," I said.

"Yes. This also my plan is being."

But when Raz tried to start the skimmer, he got hit with some more of that restricted access nonsense.

"This is new," I said.

"Yes. And not good," observed Raz.

"... access is restricted to those with level two or higher clearance," the skimmer was saying. "Do you have such clearance?"

"Yes," said Raz.

"You do?" I said.

"Yes."

"Great. So let's go. Those guards are almost here."

Actually, that wasn't even close to being true. The guards, although they were hurrying, had only covered about 10 yards, leaving them still 40 yards away. Those big tails swinging back and forth definitely slowed them down. If they were my guards, I'd make them cut off their tails and then I'd teach them how to run.

"Name and code name, please," said the computer.

"Name, An-zo Raz. Code name, uh, ..."

"What's the matter?" I said. "Don't you remember it?"

"It's, uh, just ..." Raz's normal peach-colored complexion had darkened to almost red, and he looked terribly embarrassed.

"Are you blushing?" I said.

"Code name, please," said the computer.

"It's ... it's Hula Boy," said Raz.

"Hula Boy? Your code name is Hula Boy?" I said. My grin was so big my face hurt.

"Yes, I am Hula Boy," said Raz.

I couldn't help it - I busted out laughing It wasn't really that funny, but I guess I just needed temporary relief from the constant tension I'd been under. Raz, however, apparently didn't think it was that funny. His face got darker and darker - whether from embarrassment or anger, I wasn't sure. Just to be on the safe side, though, I apologized for laughing at him.

"How may I assist you, Mr. An-zo?" said the skimmer.

"Get us out of here as quickly as you can," Raz said.

In retrospect, and from my point of view, this was not a particularly good way of telling the skimmer we were in a hurry to leave. Suddenly, without any warning, we shot straight forward and then up at a tremendous rate of acceleration. I was slammed back in the seat, and my butt was jammed into the tail tube.

We leveled off at about 1,000 feet. I tried to wriggle myself free from the tail tube but didn't have much luck - I was folded in half, with my thighs and body wedged tight in the tube and only my arms, lower legs, shoulders and head free.

"Stuck?" said Raz, observing me thrashing around, trying to free myself.

"Yes."

He offered me a hand and helped me extricate myself, all the while grinning broadly.

"It's not that funny, Hula Boy," I said.

"Yes, it is," said Raz, and laughed.

I ignored him. "All right, to the country house," I said. "Do you know the route?"

"The skimmer is knowing." Raz gave instructions to the skimmer and we settled back and made ourselves comfortable for the flight, which I estimated would take about an hour. Actually, settled back is what Raz did - I made myself as comfortable as possible while sitting on the front half of my seat. No sense flirting with the tail tube again, I figured.

My mind wandered from thoughts of Donna to thoughts of the missing Da-mo family to strange, out-of-context thoughts, such as, maybe one of the reasons Podoks like to travel so much is because it's the only chance they ever get to sit down and take a load off their feet. Almost all forms of transportation use the tail tube system, because it's considered too dangerous to ride around in the leaning-on-tail position. Eventually, though, my mind wandered back to our current situation.

"Do you think they'll follow us? Or send missiles to shoot us down? Something like that?" I asked Raz.

"I am not knowing," Raz said, looking concerned.

"Let's be careful, anyway."

"Yes, to be careful," he agreed.

Raz instructed the skimmer to monitor all traffic within 300 kilometers and to keep us informed of any that might be moving our way at a high rate of speed. He also told it to listen in to all military communications channels and report any instances of hearing our names or those of the royal family. Then he put his favorite news station up on the skimmer's video screen, and we watched a replay of General Noz-ti's news conference.

According to the extremely excited Podok announcer, the general was only a couple of minutes into his speech when he was interrupted by several demonstrators, one of whom appeared to be Her Royal Highness, Princess Da-mo Sesu. The princess claimed General Noz-ti had kidnapped - and perhaps even murdered - her family and was attempting to take control of the government by force. No one seemed to know exactly what happened next, but several shots were fired into the air by members of the Tetepu military, and the news conference ended in chaos.

"Wow!" I said as we watched the princess do her stuff. "She started a riot." Actually, what was happening on the screen looked like a cross between a riot and a slow-motion stampede, as the sound of gunfire sent those present at the news conference scurrying for cover.

"Yes. This is good, no?"

"I think it is," I said. "I hope the princess got away all right."

"Yes," said Raz, looking concerned.

Our worries were almost immediately eased by the announcer, who claimed the demonstrator identified as Princess Sesu was on her way to the station to give him an exclusive interview.

"Well, I guess that means she's all right," I said.

"Yes," said Raz. "So it is seeming."

We spent the rest of the flight watching various news stations, trying to get more information, but each station was giving out pretty much the same story - demonstrators, shots fired, panic, and stay tuned for an exclusive live interview with the leader of the demonstrators, Princess Sesu, who was on her way to the station even as the announcer gave us this news.

"Do you think the princess promised an exclusive interview to every station in town?" I said.

"Probably so," Raz said.

"Do you think she'll show up for any of them?"

"I am not knowing. Maybe better is not to be showing."

"Yeah, you could be right. If she goes on the news live, Nasty's troops will know exactly where to find her."

"This is not good."

"Let's hope she's smart enough to just go somewhere and hide. Maybe back to Slar's."

"To be hoping," Raz agreed.

The computer interrupted us with the news we were approaching the Da-mo country estate, and asked for instructions.

"Whaddaya think?" I said to Raz. "A flyover?"

"Yes," said Raz. "This is good." He gave instructions to the computer and we made a slow pass over the property at 1,000 meters.

"See anything?" I said.

"No."

"Me, neither."

We made another pass at 500 meters, but didn't see anything from that altitude, either.

"No one here is being," Raz said.

"They could just be in the house," I said. "It's not like they'd be expecting us." And, of course, skimmers are so quiet they'd never have heard us passing overhead, if, indeed, they were in the house.

"So? What to be doing?"

I pointed out a spot, just over a knoll that couldn't be seen from the main house. "Put her down over there," I said.

Raz switched control of the skimmer from autofly to manual and landed us in the place I'd indicated. We bounced a couple of times, but overall it was a pretty good landing. I opened my door and climbed out.

"I'll go check things out," I said. "You wait here. If anything goes wrong, you get out of here. Okay?"

"I am also to be going," Raz said, starting to open his door.

"No, really, Raz. You wait here. I can do this more easily alone."

"Really?"

"Sure. I'll sneak up to the house and take a look around. If there are guards, or troops, or anything weird, I'll come back and we'll make some kind of new plan."

Raz didn't say anything, but he had a sort of dubious look on his face.

"I will. I promise," I said. "Look, I'm light on my feet, quiet and fast. This will be easy. I'll be back in no time at all."

"All right."

I closed my door and headed for the house, skirting the shed where Princess Sesu and I had been held captive the year before, then dropping to my hands and knees to crawl the last 50 yards up to the house. By the time I got there, I was totally out of breath and nearly exhausted. I paused in the bushes to the left of the front door, taking deep breaths and resting.

Up until now, all this had been just an exercise. I mean, so far there had been no signs of life, and for all I knew I was sneaking up on an empty house. But then I heard, coming from inside, the sounds of voices.

The nearest window was about 10 feet away. I crawled over to it and very carefully peeked inside. No one was in the room, but the voices were louder. They seemed to be coming from the back of the house, where several outboard rooms were connected to the main part of the house by short, roofed, but otherwise open pathways, or breezeways.

I crawled along the building until I came to the first of these breezeways. No one was in sight, and the doors to both the main house and the outboard room were closed, so I elected to cut through the breezeway rather than crawl around the perimeter. I climbed over the low railing that marked the edge of the path, and started across.

I'm not entirely sure about what happened next. I remember hearing a noise, off to my left, and turning to look, but I never completed my turn. Something big and heavy hit me in the side of the head, knocking me over the railing and robbing me of my consciousness. The last thing I remember thinking, just before the blackness closed in, was that I was the human who saves the life of Podoks, and this shouldn't be happening to me.

Chapter 15

"Roger? Roger? Are you all right?"

Someone was lightly slapping my face. I pushed his hands away and opened my eyes. Blue sky and *ma-pa*, Pode's yellow sun, rushed in to replace the darkness and temporarily blind me.

"He's awake," said a voice from above me.

Just for a second I thought I might be dead, and I was waking up on the 'other side,' but then I put my hand up and blocked ma-pa's rays from shining directly into my eyes. A couple of feet above me, looking extremely concerned, was a slightly-out-of-focus Podok face. "Prince Stee?" I said.

"Oh, Roger, I'm so glad you're awake," he said, helping me to a sitting position. "I thought you might be ... you know."

"How long was I out?"

"Just briefly. But enough to give us all a scare."

I looked around and forced my eyes to focus. Standing behind the prince, also looking worried, were Emperor Fen and Empress Nememe. "What happened, anyway?" I said.

"I'm so sorry," Prince Stee said. "I didn't know it was you."

"What did you hit me with?" I said, beginning to get a picture of what had happened to me.

"My tail," Prince Stee said, a little sheepishly. "I slapped you with my tail."

"Why? Who did you think I was?"

"I didn't know."

"Then why did you hit me?"

"It's Raz's fault."

"Raz?"

"Yes. He's been my teacher, as well as my bodyguard. And he always said, when you're in a dangerous situation, shoot first and ask questions later. So when I opened the door and saw you standing there with your back to me, I just reacted. I'm sorry, Roger, really I am."

"Well, it's a good thing you didn't have a gun, I guess." It was also a good thing it was Prince Stee who had slapped me, and not some *mak su* expert, like Raz. If that had happened, I'd be dead right now.

"Yes, I probably would have shot you."

"I'm going to have to talk to Raz about this 'shoot first' policy of his." With Prince Stee's assistance, I struggled to my feet. I was still a little woozy.

"We're also sorry, Roger," Emperor Fen said.

"Yes," said Empress Nememe. "We would feel terrible if anything happened to you. Why, you're just like a son to us, Roger. Our pale-skinned son with no tail."

I couldn't help but smile at Empress Nememe's comments - she sounded so ... so ... motherly. "Thank you, Your Highness," I said. "But I'm fine - I think. What about the three of you? Are you all okay?"

"Physically, yes," said Emperor Fen. "But I am so angry. When I get a hold of General Noz-ti, I'll ... I'll ... well, I don't know what I'll do, but I'll think of something, you can count on that."

I was about to bring up Princess Sesu's favorite revenge - slow roasting over an open flame - but before I could mention it, Prince Stee interrupted me.

"Have you seen Sesu?"

"Yes, she's fine," I said. "And she's been very useful to both Raz and me. She even helped us escape from the dungeon."

"You were in the dungeon?" said Prince Stee.

"Yeah. They were going to execute Raz and me, but your sister got us out."

"I'm not surprised," said Emperor Fen. "She's a tough one."

"Roger, how did you get here?" said Empress Nememe.

"Oh." I'd forgotten about Raz. "Raz and I came in your skimmer - the big one. We stole it from the garage while General Noz-ti was holding a news conference."

"Raz is here, too?" said Prince Stee.

"Yes. The skimmer's parked just over that little hill past the shed. I made him wait while I checked this place out - we weren't sure about who was here."

"General Noz-ti held a news conference?" said the emperor. "What did he say?"

"Well, not much. Your daughter interrupted him before he could say much of anything. But he was planning to say you were in hiding and had temporarily put him in charge of the government - he even has the Imperial Passes you gave to Raz and me, and he's claiming that as proof you want him in charge."

"Ooh, ..." Emperor Fen was so angry he couldn't speak.

"Perhaps we'd better go find Raz and get out of here," I said. "Is there anything you need to take with us?"

"No," said the emperor. "We're ready right now."

"Good. Then let's go." I started toward the skimmer, and the other three fell in alongside me. "The sooner we get back to Tapu, the sooner we can put an end to all this 'taking-over-the-government' nonsense."

"Yes. I knew it was a good move on my part when I put you on this case," said Emperor Fen.

"Don't forget Raz," I said.

"Yes, of course. You and Raz. I knew what I was doing when I enlisted your help."

"Thank you," I said. "I appreciate your confidence in us." Undeserved though it may be, I thought.

We had gone only a few steps when a dark shadow passed over us. I looked up, expecting, I guess, to find Raz had tired of waiting and was conducting another flyover, trying to find out why I'd been gone so long. Instead, hovering in the air a couple of hundred meters above us was a large dark blue skimmer of the Tetepuan Defense Force.

"They must have followed us," I said. "C'mon, let's get back in the house."

As if to encourage us to do just that, the military skimmer launched a volley of laser shots that tore up the ground a couple of yards in front of us. We took the hint, turning and running back toward the shelter of the house. At least, I ran - I don't know about my three friends. What I do know is they arrived at the house only a half-step behind me, which had to make them the three fastest Podoks on Pode.

"What about Raz?" Prince Stee said, as we crouched at a window, looking out.

"He'll see them," I said. "I just hope he sees them before they see him."

"He will," said Prince Stee. "I'm sure of it."

Suddenly, as if to confirm Prince Stee's faith in him, Raz's skimmer shot skyward at a tremendous speed, passing the military skimmer and continuing upward until it disappeared into some hazy clouds. It was pretty much the same maneuver that had jammed my butt into the tail tube when we'd left the palace.

The military skimmer fired several laser shots after Raz, but didn't even come close to hitting him.

"He saw them," I said. As always, I was good at pointing out the obvious.

"Yes. And now he has the advantage," said Prince Stee. "That military skimmer is a target just waiting to be hit."

Evidently Raz thought so, too. As we watched, the big blue and gold skimmer of Emperor Fen, piloted by Raz, came swooping out of the clouds in a big arc, its laser cannons on full fire.

"I didn't know your skimmer was armed with lasers," I said to Emperor Fen.

He looked surprised. "You didn't think the leader of the largest country on Pode would travel in an unarmed ship, did you?"

"I guess not, now that I think about it."

"All my skimmers have the very latest in technology," said the emperor. "Including weapons."

We turned our attention back to the sky. Raz had leveled off and was heading straight for the military skimmer, lasers blazing. It looked as if it was going to be a short battle.

Unfortunately for Raz, and for us, too, I guess, Prince Stee was wrong in his assessment of the military skimmer. It was not 'a target just waiting to be hit.' In fact, as Raz's skimmer approached, the military skimmer took off at high speed, heading straight toward Raz, lasers on full fire.

"What are they doing?" I said, alarmed, as the two skimmers headed straight for each other. "Are they trying to crash into each other?"

"Don't worry," said Prince Stee. "The skimmers won't let that happen."

"But Raz is an inexperienced skimmer pilot. Will he know what to do?"

"It's pretty much automatic. All he has to do is hang on and fire the weapons."

"You're sure?"

"Watch." He pointed as the two skimmers, twisting and turning and performing evasive maneuvers that would have been impossible with any other kind of aircraft, passed within a few meters of each other at extremely high speeds.

Although the thought bothered me, I was glad I was where I was, on the ground, instead of up there with Raz, where I should have been, fighting the enemy. But I knew my stomach wouldn't have been able to take the kinds of maneuvers Raz was making. Just one rollover or an upside-down anything would have had me barfing all over the cabin, not exactly what Raz needed at this critical time. So I mentally crossed my fingers and hoped for the best as the drama in the sky played itself out.

The two skimmers made big sweeping turns at opposite ends of the sky, then headed back toward each other. When they got into each other's range, they began firing their laser cannons, at the same time trying to avoid being hit by enemy fire. It was a spectacular sight, made slightly comical by the way each skimmer seemed to be wriggling back and forth across the other's path as it approached.

"Come on, Raz!" Prince Stee shouted as the two skimmers once again passed each other at close - *very* close - range. And then to me he said, "This is very exciting, don't you think?"

"Considering our lives probably depend on the outcome, I guess you're right," I said. Still, there was something about the lack of noise accompanying the skimmer fight that tended to keep the excitement level at less than maximum, at least for me. I mean, you couldn't hear the skimmers at all, and the laser cannons made little sissy pinging noises when they were fired, not at all like the loud thuds and boom that came from the troop carrier when it was chasing us. Somewhere deep inside, I longed for the roar and rat-a-tat-tat of more-conventional weapons.

By the time the skimmers had charged each other six or seven times, the thrill had pretty much worn off. The whole thing reminded me of jousting, and it seemed neither Raz nor his adversary could knock the other off his horse. I was just about to tell Prince Stee and the others about all this - jousting, I mean - when Raz scored the first and, as it turned out, only hit.

Even that was disappointing. Instead of a fireball exploding in the sky, there was some slight sparking around the edge of the military skimmer, and then it seemed to lose control. It turned onto one edge and dropped from the sky, crashing too far away for us to see it hit the ground.

Raz made one more sweeping turn and then landed the skimmer in the front yard, where the four of us were waiting for him. He exited, looking flushed but smiling, and immediately approached Emperor Fen, whom he saluted.

"That was wonderful, Raz!" Prince Stee said. "You were magnificent up there!" He was about as excited as I'd ever seen him.

"Thank you, Your Highness," Raz said.

"I wish I'd been up there with you," said the prince.

"Yeah. Me, too," I lied.

Raz gave me a smile as if he could read my mind. I smiled back, knowing he couldn't.

"Excellent work, Raz," said Emperor Fen. "I can't thank you enough."

"No thank yous are necessary, Your Highness. This is my job."

"Well, thank you, anyway, Raz," said Empress Nememe. "Thank you for doing your job so well."

Raz's face started to show some reddening, and I knew he was embarrassed, so I jumped into the conversation to save him. "We'd better go," I said. "There could be others on the way."

"Yes, you're right," said the emperor. "Let's get out of here while we can."

We got aboard the skimmer and took off, climbing quickly into the afternoon sky as the Da-mo country home faded from view behind us. Prince Stee and his father watched it for a while, then settled back for the return flight to Tapu.

"We would have died there, you know," said Empress Nememe.

"If it hadn't been for you two," said Prince Stee.

"It's true," said the emperor. "There was no food, no water, no communications gear - nothing! We would have died."

"Well, we're glad you didn't," I said, speaking for both Raz and myself. Even as I said it, I realized how stupid it sounded. But, of course, as always, it was too late.

"Once again, the human who saves the lives - " Prince Stee started to say, but I cut him off.

"Wait a minute! Wait a minute. Are you forgetting? It was Raz who rescued you, not me."

"Yes, that's right," said the emperor. "And Raz, you will be rewarded for this heroic behavior."

"Thank you, Your Highness," Raz said, and started to turn red again.

"So, listen up, everyone," I said. "We need to make some plans, and we need to do it now. If we just go cruising into Tapu like this, we're likely to be shot out of the sky."

There were murmurs of assent.

"And what are we going to do when we get there?" I said, continuing. "It's probably not safe to go back to the palace. We need to go someplace else and carry out our plans - whatever they are - from there."

"Well, let's look at the news and see what's happening," said the emperor. "Then we can make our plans based on that."

It sounded like a good idea, but when we attempted to tune in a news channel, we couldn't get one. All of them - over 10 stations, according to Prince Stee - were showing the same picture of Emperor Fen, along with some writing I couldn't read, and nothing else.

"What does it say?" I asked Prince Stee.

"Please stand by. We'll be back shortly."

"I should have known. Just like on Earth, when things go wrong."

Emperor Fen reached out and touched my arm. "Roger, we need someone to be in charge of this ... this little ... expedition of ours, and I want it to be you. Is that all right?"

"Well, yes, Your Highness. If that's what you want."

"It is."

It wasn't as if I really had a choice in the matter - what the emperor wants, he usually gets - so I agreed.

"So, Roger, what is your plan?" said Prince Stee.

It was a good question. I'd agreed to lead them out of this mess we were in, and now they wanted to know the details. Fair enough. The only problem was, my mind was a blank and I really had no idea at all of what to do next.

Chapter 16

Okay. I needed a plan and I needed it in a hurry. On other, similar occasions when I've been in situations like this - that is, expected to come up with something when I was completely out of ideas - I've found the best way to stall is to ask questions. So that's what I did.

"Before I tell you my plan," I said, "I need to clear up a couple of things."

"What?" said Prince Stee.

"Well, for one thing, are you aware of anyone following us, Raz, while we were on our way here?"

"No."

"Then where did that military skimmer come from? How did they know where we were?"

"Maybe they were nearby and saw us arrive," Raz said.

"Or maybe they were just checking up on us - my parents and myself, I mean - and accidentally bumped into you two, as well," Prince Stee offered. "There's a military skimmer unit about 150 or 200 kilometers from here."

"I suppose that's possible," I said. "But I think they're tracking us."

"Tracking us?" said Emperor Fen.

"Sure. They know we took this skimmer. It has a transponder, doesn't it?"

"Yes, of course."

"It would be pretty easy to keep track of us, then," I said.

Everyone seemed to agree on that point.

"So what should we do?" said the emperor.

"Can't we turn it off?" said Empress Nememe.

"Can we?" I said to Raz.

"Maybe. Let me ask the skimmer."

Apparently the skimmer had been listening in our conversation, because, without waiting for the question to be asked, the smooth female voice informed us deactivating the transponder would be a violation of several national laws and, in any case, could only be accomplished while the skimmer was on the ground, not in the air.

"So, what should we do?" said Prince Stee.

There was that question again, but this time I was ready. "Raz, you see those three mountains over there? The three tall ones sticking up above the others?"

"Yes."

"Head for the middle one. And take us down low. Really low, so we're just skimming the tops of the trees."

"All right." Raz banked the skimmer slightly and we changed direction, heading for the three mountain peaks off in the distance, and at the same time beginning to descend to treetop level.

"Isn't this a little out of our way?" said Prince Stee.

"Yes, it is," I said. "This is the way I want to do it."

"What's over there by those mountains, anyway?"

"The Valley of the Ancients."

"Really?" said the emperor.

"Yes, Your Highness. Really."

"Then this is how you and Sesu came? Last year?"

"Yes. The same way."

"What are we going to do when we get to the mountains?" said Raz.

"We're going to go down into the valley and land."

"Land?" said the emperor. "Do you think that's wise? What if they catch us on the ground?"

"We'll be in trouble. But I've decided we need to remove the transponder if we're going to get back to Tapu safely. And we have to land to do that."

"I see," said the emperor.

"So, is it all right? To land, I mean."

"Yes, yes. Of course. You're in charge."

"They could also be tracking us by the computer," said Raz. "All the palace skimmers are on the same network."

"Then we'll have to disable that," I said. "And you'll have to fly us out of here manually."

"I can do that," Raz said with a grin.

"Good." I grinned back at him. "I'm counting on it."

When we got to the mountains, Raz slowed the skimmer and took us down into the Valley of the Ancients. It looked pretty much the same as when Raz and I were here recently - steep-sided walls with a wide, grass-covered valley floor, and the Tapu River flowing down the center toward Tapu. I didn't really expect it to look any different.

"So this is where you and my daughter spent all that time together?" said Empress Nememe.

"Yes, Your Highness. This is it."

"It's beautiful. No wonder Sesu talks about it all the time."

I pointed out a couple of familiar-looking spots to Prince Stee and his folks as we followed the river down the valley, heading toward Tapu. I also reminded Raz to watch out for fotods, those strange creatures with the built-in gas bags that float up and down the valley on the winds. Of course, Raz had been in the valley before and knew all about fotods, but it never hurts to be careful.

Eventually we came to the spot I'd been looking for - a large, tight cluster of tall, leafy trees right next to the river.

"Park her there, Raz," I said, pointing. "Under the trees."

Raz slowed the skimmer to nearly a hover and guided us to a smooth landing beneath the grove of trees.

"Perfect landing, Raz," I said, patting him on the back as we settled to a stop. "I couldn't have done better, myself."

"You mean, you couldn't have done as well, don't you?" Raz said.

"Well, maybe. Let's hope you handle this thing just as well after we disable the computer."

"Also to be hoping," Raz said, quietly, under his breath, in English. Obviously, this comment was intended for me only.

We climbed out of the skimmer and assembled in a group next to it. The other four all looked at me expectantly. It was clear what they wanted - they wanted to hear the rest of my plan.

"Okay," I began. "This is what we're going to do. Everyone stays here, under the trees, while Raz works on the skimmer. That way, if anyone flies over, they won't be able to spot us just accidentally - they'll have to have all their equipment turned on and be actively looking for us. Also, no matter how long it takes to remove the transponder and disable the computer, we're going to stay here until it gets dark."

"Until dark?" said Prince Stee. "Is that really necessary?"

"Maybe, maybe not. We have no way of finding out what the situation in Tapu is right now. And after we disable the computer, we'll be completely cut off. So, just to be on the safe side, we'll remain here until dark, and then head back to Tapu."

"Do you have a plan for after we get back?" said the emperor.

"I have a plan for what to do first, when we get there, but what happens after that depends entirely on the situation. Without knowing what's going on, exactly, it's impossible to decide on a course of action."

"Of course," said Prince Stee. "That makes sense."

"So when we get to Tapu, we'll go to Slar's house and see if we can find out anything there," I said. "If not, we'll come up with another plan. Okay?"

"Slar's house?" said Emperor Fen.

"Dee-pok Slar, Princess Sesu's driver. He's been helping us," I explained.

The four Podoks all agreed with my plan, and Raz set to work removing the transponder and disconnecting the computer. The four of us settled in a few feet away - they leaning on their tails and me sitting on a rock.

"You know," Emperor Fen said, "I can't really believe all this is happening. And General Noz-ti, of all Podoks - it's especially hard to believe he's responsible."

"It's not hard for me," Empress Nememe said. "I never liked him - always bossing the palace help around like he was some kind of, of ..."

"Big shot," I said.

"Yes. Exactly," said the empress. "A big shot, that's what he was."

"Well, he's sealed his fate," said Emperor Fen. "When I get back, I'll take care of him."

"You know, Your Highness, it might not be that easy to regain control of your government," I said. "General Noz-ti seems to have the support of many, if not most, of the Tetepuan Defense Force. If he decides to force a confrontation, it could be a difficult battle."

"Don't you believe it, Roger," Prince Stee said. "The great majority of my father's troops are loyal to him, and to no one else. General Noz-ti has tricked them into believing what's going on is at the bidding of my father."

"I have to agree with my son on that point," Emperor Fen said. "General Noz-ti isn't well-liked by his troops, according to my understanding. If it came to a choice, I'm sure they'd choose me."

"Well, I hope you're both right," I said. "But he may not be presenting them with that exact choice."

"What do you mean?" said Empress Nememe. "What other choices are there?"

"He may be presenting this as a choice between having Tetepu continue as an empire or switching to democratic rule."

"He wouldn't do that," said the emperor. "He wants to be in charge."

"I'm sure you're right. But he could be lying - promising democracy when he really intends just to take over. That's the way they do it on Earth."

"That sounds like something he might do," said Prince Stee.

"In any case, I just wanted to point out it might not be as easy as walking into the palace and announcing your return."

"I guess we'll be finding out shortly," said Emperor Fen. "Ma-pa is already starting to set."

I looked up at the yellow Pode sun, which was just beginning to dip below the steep-sided walls of the valley, across the river. "Yeah, I guess we will," I said.

Raz finished working on the skimmer and joined our little discussion group.

"Everything okay, Raz?" I said.

"Yes. I shut down the computer and removed the transponder. They won't be able to track us now."

"So, the only other thing we have to worry about is ground radar," said Prince Stee. "Without the transponder signal, they'll automatically classify us as a threat and send someone up to see who we are."

"We'll just have to stay so low that radar can't pick us up," I said.

"Even if they send someone up to investigate," said Empress Nememe, "they'll see it's our skimmer and know it's us, won't they?"

I shook my head. "I don't think so. As far as the Tetepuan Defense Force knows, Raz and I were in on the assassination attempt, and we escaped by stealing this skimmer. Their orders are probably to shoot on sight."

"Oh, that's not so good, then."

"No, it's not," agreed her husband.

"I really hope Sesu is safe," Empress Nememe said. "I'm worried about her - she thinks she's indestructible."

I was worried about the princess, too, and had been ever since we split up, but my worries hadn't seemed like a good thing to bring out into the open, so I'd kept them to myself. However, once the empress brought it up - broke the ice, so to speak - the rest of us were free to reveal our feelings. And so we did. All of us, it seemed, were secretly concerned about what might have happened to Princess Sesu.

"I wish there were some way to contact her, to send her a message," said the empress.

Everyone - even me - nodded in agreement, with Prince Stee adding a "Me, too," for emphasis.

"But we can't," I said. "Any message we send will automatically reveal our location. So we'll just have to trust that she and her friends are okay, and they were completely successful in disrupting General Noz-ti's plans to hold a news conference."

Murmurs of assent and a couple of yeahs followed, and talk of the princess and any trouble she might be in trailed off. And while I didn't say anything to the others, my own inner worries were somewhat tempered by my belief that Princess Sesu was more than able to take care of herself.

We spent the rest of the daylight hours making small talk, or, as we say in Hawaii, *talking story*. The emperor and empress were quite interested in hearing about Hawaii, and I answered dozens of questions about our weather, and our food, and our flowers, and our music, and numerous other subjects. I got the distinct impression the Da-mo family - or the emperor and empress, at least - were thinking about visiting our small islands at some point in the future.

The afternoon wore on without interruption from the outside world. At one point Emperor Fen started telling jokes, but most of them weren't very funny and the laughter that followed sounded forced, so he soon gave it up. His best joke went like this - Question - What happens at a Podok ballet recital? Answer - The biggest Podok wins. I had to think about it a bit - picture it in my mind, actually - but once I got it, I thought it was pretty funny. The rest of his jokes were nowhere near as good, but they did help us pass the time. And then, almost without our realizing it, daylight was gone and darkness had replaced it.

"It's time to go," I said.

The lighthearted mood present for much of the afternoon disappeared and was replaced by a more somber one as we climbed into the skimmer and took off, headed for Tapu. All of us seemed to realize just how important this mission was - there was no room for failure, only success was acceptable. We had to restore the emperor to his rightful position as ruler of Tetepu.

Raz kept the skimmer low and followed the river, which was easy to see in the moonlight. Not having the computer's help made his piloting a little on the ragged side at first, but in a short while he got the hang of it. By the time we got to the Tapu city limits, he was doing just as well without the computer as he'd done with it.

"Should we go around the city?" Raz asked me. "Or just head directly for Slar's house from here?"

"What do you think?"

"Quicker is better, in my opinion. And a straight line is always the quickest way."

"Let's do it like that, then. The sooner we get out of the sky and into a nice, safe house, the better I'll feel."

Raz banked the skimmer and headed out across the city toward Slar's. We were only a few minutes away, but in my opinion, those few minutes represented the most dangerous part of our trip. If we were going to get caught, here inside the city limits is where it was likely to happen. As is my habit when faced with stressful situations such as this, I mentally crossed my fingers and wished for luck.

Chapter 17

I needn't have worried. Our low-altitude flight across the city was completely uneventful, and we arrived at Slar's without incident. Just to be on the safe side, though, we parked the skimmer in a children's tailball field about two blocks away, and walked the rest of the way to the house.

Slar's house was all lit up, and cars and skimmers - some of them adorned with the logos of local news stations - littered the front yard and the street beyond. As we got close we could hear, from inside the house, what appeared to be dozens of Podoks engaged in conversations, and an occasional loud whooping noise in a voice sounding suspiciously like Princess Sesu's.

"Looks like they're having a party," I said, as we walked up to the front door.

"Just wait until they see us," said Prince Stee. "They're going to go wild." He pulled open the door and we went in.

At first, no one seemed to notice us. That wasn't really a surprise, because Slar's front room was so packed with partying Podoks it was impossible to see more than a foot or two. But then a whisper began, then the whisper became a buzz, and then the buzz became ... silence. Complete silence. The wall of Podoks in front of us parted, as if by magic, and there, standing on the other side of the room, just turning to see what had caused the party to go suddenly flat, was Princess Sesu.

"Daddy! Mommy!" she shouted, and hurried across the room to embrace her parents. "We knew you were okay, but I'm so glad to see you. You, too, Stee. And Roger and Raz, what can I say? I knew you could do it." She hugged each of us, in turn, as the crowd watched.

"How did you know we were safe?" Emperor Fen said.

"You see this crowd?" Princess Sesu said. "These are the Podoks who helped me. They're all in the news business, with excellent contacts - we heard all about the big skimmer battle at the country house almost as soon as it happened, because the crew of the skimmer that Raz shot down sent out a distress call and said you had managed to escape. We've just been waiting for you to show up."

So, the crew of the TDF skimmer had survived the crash – I guess anti-gravity had something to do with that – and let everyone know we were safe and on our way. I suddenly understood why all those news channels were off the air. Nobody was at the stations - everyone was here, partying.

The emperor took a couple of steps into the center of the room. The crowd, which had been watching us in near silence, grew even more quiet as Emperor Fen looked around the room at them.

"I just want to thank all of you," he said, "for helping my daughter, and also for supporting me and my family in this difficult time. Please, continue with your celebration. Enjoy yourselves."

The emperor's impromptu little speech was followed by an awkward moment of silence, and then someone banged his tail on the floor, which is the Podok equivalent of clapping. A couple of others joined in, and soon the entire room was shaking from the effect of all those tails being banged on Slar's floor. It felt like an earthquake, or perhaps I should say a *podequake*.

And with that, the party resumed. Several of those present were recordists, and they had recorded the entire confrontation with General Noz-ti. One by one they played their recordings on Slar's video screen, while Emperor Fen, Empress Nememe and Prince Stee watched. Raz and I went into the kitchen to talk.

"Not to be finished," Raz said, after he had cleared the room of party guests.

"I know. This is just a temporary victory."

"Yes."

"As long as Nasty is still running around free, we can't relax. We've got to find him and put him away."

"This is good, but how to be doing?"

"I guess we'll have to go to the palace and confront him."

Raz looked thoughtful.

"What?" I said.

"We are too small being."

"Too small?"

"Yes. We are only two being. General Nasty is much support having."

"Actually, I think most of the guards and military who are supporting him don't really know what's going on. They honestly believe the emperor put him in charge."

"Still, they are on his side being."

"Then we've got to convince them they're on the wrong side."

"You are a plan having?"

"Well, I like what Princess Sesu did to Nasty- confronted him with half the media in Tapu, cameras and recorders capturing the whole thing. I think we should do the same, only this time we'll have the entire royal family with us. When they see Emperor Fen, and hear him call Nasty a liar, they'll understand what's really going on."

"This is for Emperor Fen most dangerous being," Raz said.

"Well, that's true. But I can't think of any other way to do it. Can you?"

Raz didn't answer.

"If you've got a better plan, I'm listening," I said.

Before Raz could reply - if he was going to - the kitchen door swung open and we were joined by Prince Stee. "What are you two doing in here?" he said.

"We're trying to figure out what to do next," I told him.

"You have a plan?"

I looked at Raz, and he gave me a slight nod of his head. "Our plan is to move this party back to the palace and confront General Noz-ti again. This time with your whole family present to denounce him."

"Aren't you afraid his followers might just shoot us all? Then there would be no one to stop him."

"I suppose that is a possibility," I admitted. "But I'm not so sure he has that many loyal followers. I think most of the palace guards and military troops are loyal to your father, and Nasty has tricked them into helping him. When they see you and your family, and hear about Nasty's treachery from your father's own mouth, they'll be on our side."

"With a few exceptions," Raz said.

"How many is a few?" said Prince Stee.

I shrugged. "We don't know. It might be 10, it might be 50. In any case, we'll probably outnumber them."

"Outnumber, yes. But they'll have weapons. All we'll have are cameras and recorders."

I resisted the urge to trot out that old cliche about the recorder being mightier than any weapon, and said instead, "We're open to suggestions, if you've got a better idea."

"I don't," Prince Stee said, after thinking about it for a while. "Let me go talk to my father and see what he says."

"All right."

"When would we be doing this?"

"I don't see any reason to wait. Do you, Raz?"

"No. The sooner, the better."

Prince Stee left to get his father's opinion of our plan. He was gone only a second or two when the kitchen door swung open again. This time our visitor was Princess Sesu.

"What's going on in here?" she said. "Don't you like parties?"

I told her what we were planning to do.

"I like it," she said. "It's simple and direct."

"It could be dangerous," Raz pointed out. "General Noz-ti and his supporters could shoot us all."

"I doubt that," said the princess. "And he certainly has less support now than he did earlier. Everyone saw what happened when I challenged him at the news conference."

"Well, in any case, it's up to your father," I said.

"Oh, he'll be in favor of your plan. I guarantee it. Let me go talk to him."

"I am for to be much worrying," Raz said, after Princess Sesu had left.

"About what?" I said.

"Emperor Fen. This is not emperor work - too dangerous being."

"Look, Raz. This is his empire that Nasty is trying to overthrow. If the emperor isn't willing to take a little risk to get it back, then I don't see why I should. Or you, either, for that matter."

Raz's face turned angry. I guess, because of his job, he wasn't used to thinking of the royal family in this manner.

I waited, saying nothing, and after a short while his features softened and the angry look disappeared.

"Yes," he said. "Emperor Fen must be also helping."

"Good, I'm glad you agree. For a minute there I thought you were going to hit me when I suggested it. Or even worse, bite me," I said, intending the last part as a joke.

Raz looked hurt. "Raz is never for to be Roger hurting," he said. "Always friends being."

"I'm sorry, Raz. You're right. Friends forever."

The door opened and Emperor Fen, Empress Nememe, Prince Stee, Princess Sesu, and about half of the party guests came into the kitchen. "We're ready," said the emperor, speaking, I assumed, for everyone.

"Are you sure?" I asked Emperor Fen. "This could be dangerous. There could be shooting, there could be casualties."

Emperor Fen turned toward his supporters. "Are we afraid?" he said.

"NO!" yelled the crowd, so loud the earpiece of my vox-box began to vibrate inside my ear, producing an unpleasant tickling sensation.

"Well, that sounds definite enough," I said with a smile. "Let's get going."

With some effort and a lot of noise, Raz and I got everyone assembled outside the house on Slar's lawn. I stood on Slar's little porch, along with Raz and Emperor Fen, and addressed the crowd.

"Okay, listen up, everyone," I began. "We want to stick together and all arrive at the palace at the same time, as one big group. That means the skimmers will have to wait for the cars. I suggest those with skimmers keep them low, under 100 meters, say, and follow the cars. All right?"

The crowd murmured its agreement with my suggestions.

"One more thing before we leave," I said. "I want to split up the royal family - only one member to a vehicle. That way, if anything should happen, well ..."

"All right, then," said Raz. "Let's move out."

There was some minor jockeying among the news crews over who deserved the privilege of having the emperor ride with them, which was solved when Emperor Fen walked to the nearest skimmer and climbed in, and then we were on our way. Raz and I rode together in one of the news skimmers, leaving the skimmer in which we'd arrived at the park. All together, our little procession must have numbered close to 30 vehicles, of which 10 or 12 were skimmers and the rest, cars.

Raz looked perfectly calm, but my stomach was rocking and rolling with nervousness. The confidence I had tried to project to the royal family and the crowd back at Slar's was completely false - I had plenty of doubts about this so-called 'plan' of ours. Just because confronting Nasty had worked for Princess Sesu didn't mean it would work for us. In fact, that earlier confrontation would probably work against us - they were caught by surprise before, but this time they'd be ready. Still, I couldn't think of anything else we could do. Confronting General

Noz-ti was something that had to be done sooner or later, and now seemed as good a time as any.

"Not to be worrying," Raz said to me. "This plan is good."

Sometimes I think Raz can read my mind. I smiled at him. "Let's hope so," I said. "Because if it's not - you, me, all of us - we're in big trouble."

Chapter 18

The royal palace - home to the Da-mo family and, during the day, to several government offices - is situated on a large, park-like tract of land less than a mile from downtown Tapu. Leading up to it is a short, wide stretch of roadway known as the Da-mo Seka, which means the trail, or the path, of the Da-mo. The Seka, as it is popularly known, dates back over a thousand years, to when it was major link between the small-at-the-time city of Tapu and other independent cities located in the yet-to-be-organized country of Tetepu. All but about 200 yards of the seka are gone now, and the short section that remains, fronting the castle, has been paved over with plastic road-paving compound and turned into a no-vehicles-allowed security zone. It was just outside this security zone our ragged procession came to a halt.

Princess Sesu took over the job of organizing our ... well, I'd like to say we were troops, but what we really were was a mob. A great big mob of Podoks and me, all milling around, wondering what to do next. I joined Princess Sesu at the front of the group, where the rest of the royal family and Raz had also assembled. The crowd quieted down at the sight of the emperor and his family.

"Thank you, Princess," I said to her.

"I hope you don't mind," she said. "Me trying to get everyone lined up and in position, I mean."

"No, I don't mind a -"

"It's just that I've done this before," she said, cutting me off. "Just a little while ago, in fact. But I don't want to crush anyone's toes."

"What?" I said, momentarily confused.

"Isn't that right?" Princess Sesu said.

"Isn't what right?"

"If I take over your job without asking you, does that crush your toes?"

It dawned on me just what she was talking about. "It's step on," I said. "When you do something like that, you step on someone's toes."

"I see. Well, if I step on a human's toes, they'll end up crushed. Guaranteed. So I guess it means the same thing." She gave me a wide grin.

It was difficult to argue her point. "I guess so."

Princess Sesu turned her attention away from me and addressed the crowd. "IS EVERYBODY READY?" she yelled.

The crowd claimed they were, but they didn't sound particularly enthusiastic to me. I half expected Princess Sesu to follow with, "I CAN'T HEAR YOU!!" but she didn't. Instead, she turned to her parents and said softly, "How about you? Mommy, Daddy? Are you sure you want to go through with this? It's not too late to change your minds."

"We're ready," said her father. "Let's get this over with."

And with that we set off, on foot, for the castle.

So far, we hadn't seen any guards, but I had no doubt dozens of Podoks, clomping along with enough force to cause the ground beneath us to vibrate, would bring them running. I was wrong. We marched right up to the foot of the castle steps, where we stopped.

"Where is everyone?" said the emperor.

"Good question," I said. I looked up the steps and across the wide courtyard that fronted the palace entrance. No one was in sight. The lights were on and the double front doors of the palace were opened wide. Normally, there are two guards - one on each side of the entrance - but now there were none.

"Do you think it's a trap?" said Prince Stee.

"I don't know what to think." I said. "Except it's strange. Very strange. What about you, Raz?"

"It could be a trap," he said. "Or maybe General Noz-ti and those on his side have left."

"Left? But why?" said Princess Sesu.

"Because of what you did at the news conference."

"But hardly anybody even knows about that because of the news blackout."

"Those who were there know," said Raz. "And I suspect that includes many who are loyal to the royal family. So maybe General Noz-ti decided it was impossible to keep this news from getting out, and he left while he could still get away."

"That doesn't sound like General Noz-ti," said Princess Sesu. "I've never known him to back down from a fight."

"This is much, much more than a fight," said Raz. "The losers will lose their lives. And without wide support from the population, especially the military, he may have decided it would be suicide to take on the royal family. Better to wait for another time, when he's in a better position."

"That time will never come, if I have anything to say about it," said the emperor. "In the meantime, there's only one way to find out if this is a trap or not. We have to keep going."

Murmurs from the crowd indicated most of them agreed with the emperor.

"ALL RIGHT," Princess Sesu said to the crowd. "We're going in. Let's get those recorders working."

And so we headed up the steps and across the courtyard, which, in my mind, at least, is where things - bad things, like an ambush - were most likely to occur. It was the perfect spot - at least, it was from General Noz-ti's point of view. Several windows on upper floors looked down on the courtyard, and we were completely exposed as we crossed the 30 or 40 yards separating the steps from the front door. Anyone with a weapon could easily take us all out from any one of those windows.

We separated into two groups. The lead group consisted of myself, Raz, Emperor Fen, and the other three members of the Da-mo family. About 10 yards behind us came the others, their cameras and recorders busily catching every bit of what had been, so far, an uneventful assault on the palace.

"See anything?" I said to no one in particular.

Four Podoks answered, "No."

"Me, either."

"This is spooky," said Princess Sesu.

"Looks as if Raz was right," I said. "They're gone." At least, I hoped he was right - we were in no position to engage an enemy.

We were just a few steps in front of the entrance when we saw someone coming down the hall. Actually, we didn't see *someone*, we saw someone's shadow, reflected on the floor. It was a large, ominous-looking shadow, as shadows go, and it brought both our leading group and the group behind us to a halt.

"Someone's coming," I said, as usual, pointing out the obvious.

"Yes," Raz said to me. "Are you ready?"

By ready, I assumed he meant, did I have my stungun ready?

"Yeah, I'm ready," I said, withdrawing the gun from the back waistband of my jeans. Little good this will do me, I thought, if Nasty decides to attack in force.

"If anything happens, we must protect the emperor and his family," said Raz.

"I understand."

The frightening shadow grew larger and larger, and then it disappeared, to be replaced by ... by ... who was that, anyway? Was it who I thought it was?

"Welcome home, Your Highnesses," said Ten-zo Kiki, the servant girl who had brought me chili dogs and Moon Cola on my first night staying at the palace. "We've been expecting you." She bowed slightly and crossed her arms across her chest in the same manner as a military salute.

"Hello, Kiki," said Emperor Fen. "Is that true? You've been expecting us?"

"Yes, Your Highness."

"Since when?"

"Since General Noz-ti and several of his officers left."

"When did they leave?" said Raz.

"Right after the news conference. He ordered all but 10 or 12 of his men to go to their quarters and stay there, and then he and the rest left in three skimmers."

"I don't suppose you know where they were going," I said.

"No, sir, Mr. Denton. I don't think anyone knows that."

"So who's in charge of the palace now?" said the emperor.

Ten-zo Kiki looked slightly flustered. "Well, Your Highness, I guess I am."

"You? I don't mean to insult you, Kiki, but you are, after all, only a servant here in the palace."

"I know, but I'm the only one left. At least, I was until now."

"What? You're the only one left?"

"Yes, Your Highness. The troops are confined to quarters by General Noz-ti's order - I tried to get them to come out, but they wouldn't - and everyone else ran away because they expected there to be trouble here."

"They did, did they? Tell me, then, Kiki, when everyone else ran away, why did you stay? Why didn't you run away with them?"

"I don't know, Your Highness. I just thought, ... someone should be here to greet you when you returned."

"I appreciate that, Kiki," said Emperor Fen. "I really, truly appreciate it."

Kiki started turning a dark red.

"And I won't forget it."

I hated to break up the mutual admiration society that had sprung up between the emperor and Ten-zo Kiki, but we still had things to do, places to go, and bad guys to catch. "Excuse me," I said, breaking into the conversation, "but I think we should conduct a search of the palace before we go in. I wouldn't put it past General Noz-ti to leave a couple of his men behind."

"Really?" said Emperor Fen.

"Yes."

"That seems highly unlikely to me," said the emperor.

"Well, actually, it seems unlikely to me, too. But we can't afford to take the chance - we have to check. Because if he did leave men behind, their mission would be to kill you."

The emperor sucked in his breath noisily and he staggered, just slightly, to one side. Perhaps the strain of all this was becoming too much for him - after all, he did just get out of the infirmary a short while earlier.

Princess Sesu picked up on it immediately. "Are you all right, Daddy?"

"Yes, yes. I'm fine." He turned to me and said, "All right, Roger. I brought you in on this because I trust your judgment, so we'll do whatever you want. Search the palace."

"Fine. Kiki, how many troops are left?"

"I'm not sure. Maybe 20 or 25."

"Okay. We need to get them down here so they can conduct the search."

"I'll get them," volunteered Raz.

This was just what I was hoping for - that Raz would volunteer. "Great, Raz," I said. "If they give you any trouble, tell them it's an order from the emperor and if they disobey it they'll be slow roasted over an open flame."

Raz gave me a funny look, as if to say, "What? Someone give *me* trouble?" and left, going directly into the palace through the open front doors, that being the quickest way to reach the guard barracks in the back.

"Keep an eye out!" I called after him as he walked away.

In reply, without turning around, he thumped his tail twice on the ground and kept on walking.

"So what do we do?" said Princess Sesu.

"We wait," I said.

And that's what we did - we moved closer to the palace so we wouldn't be such great targets from the windows, and we waited. It didn't take long. Much sooner than I'd expected, Raz was back, bringing with him 27 members of the palace guard, those elite troops - all officers - of the Tetepuan Defense Force who provide guard services at the palace. I mention this latter piece of information because, right now, these 27 Podoks looked like anything but what they were. Many were in civilian clothes, some were wearing parts of their uniforms mixed with civilian clothes, and two had on nothing but underwear. As they formed up in the courtyard, next to us, those two looked particularly embarrassed.

"Nice outfit," Princess Sesu said to one of the underwear-clad guards, who returned her compliment by turning a beautiful scarlet color.

"Sesu!" said her father, giving her a nasty look. "Be quiet!"

The princess looked properly chagrined as she shrank back into our little group.

Emperor Fen stepped forward, looked at the ragged formation in front of him, and smiled. "I'm glad to see all of you, despite the way you are dressed," he said. "May I assume your presence here means you are still loyal to me?"

"YES, SIR!" came the enthusiastic response from all 27 Podoks.

"Good. My friend and advisor, Roger, here, tells me it would be a good idea to search the palace and make sure none of those loyal to General Noz-ti remain. Please do that for me now."

With another resounding, "YES, SIR!" the troops dispersed and headed into the palace. Without saying anything, Raz went with them.

"So now we wait," the emperor said to the rest of us.

And, once again, that's what we did. I had intended to spend this time talking to Raz about our plans for the immediate future - after all, old Nasty Noz-ti was still on the loose - but with Raz gone, I contented myself with making light conversation with the royal family. Still, in the back of my mind, I was running through what I considered to be the various options available to Raz and me.

After what seemed to me a terribly long time, Raz returned and pronounced the castle safe to enter, so we did. Most of the reporters and recordists had left by this time - the big battle had not materialized and the return of the royal family lacked the drama they needed for a good story. As for Raz, myself, and the Da-mo family, though, we were quite happy with the way things turned out.

"What now?" Emperor Fen said.

He was looking at me as he said it, so I took it upon myself to answer. "Well, Your Highness, I think you and your family should get some rest. You did just get out of the infirmary, and this has been a trying time. Although we can't be sure what's going to happen, exactly, it appears any imminent threat of a coup has passed. This would be an excellent time to rest and regain your stamina."

"And what about you?"

"Raz and I have some things to take care of."

"Yes," Raz said softly. "Loose ends, as they say."

"Fine, then. We, or I, at least, will take your advice and retire to my quarters. However, I wish you, both of you, to join me for breakfast tomorrow morning. At that time you can give me a report of your activities."

Raz looked a little stunned as we wished the royal family good night and watched them depart for their quarters, accompanied by several guards. When we were alone, he said to me, "You are also what Emperor Fen is saying to be hearing?"

"Yeah, I heard him. Breakfast, tomorrow morning."

"Yes. To be breakfast with the emperor eating. This cannot be."

"Why not?"

"I am only a guardbody being. Not to be with emperors eating."

"Heck, I'm only a teacher," I said.

"Yes, but you are the human who is always Podok lives for to be saving. This is special being."

I looked closely to see if Raz was joking, but he appeared to be serious. "C'mon, Raz, you don't believe that nonsense. Besides, the emperor can do what he wants, can't he?"

"Yes."

"Well, he wants us to join him for breakfast. It sounded like an order to me. And you know the penalty for disobeying a royal order - slow roasting over an open flame."

Raz grinned.

"In the meantime, we've got to figure out where Nasty and his boys went when they left here. We can't let him get away, or he's likely to try something like this again."

Raz's expression became serious. "You are something to be knowing?" he said.

"Well, not exactly. But do you remember what we were planning to do, before we got thrown in the dungeon?"

"I am to be sleeping planning."

"That's right. You were going to rest up for the next day, when we were planning to visit -"

"The PUFF house," Raz said, finishing my sentence.

"Yeah, the PUFF safe house. If Nasty and some of the PUFF group are in this together, maybe that's where he went. Or, if he's not there, maybe somebody will be there who knows where he is."

"Yes. This plan I am liking. To be going." He turned without waiting for my answer and headed toward the skimmer garage.

"Raz, wait," I said. "Let's take some of the guards with us, just in case. If Nasty and his men are there, we'll be badly outnumbered."

"Yes, this is good. I am guards finding." He turned and walked away, leaving me standing there alone.

"I'll meet you at the skimmer garage," I called after him.

His answer was two thumps of his tail on the palace floor, then he turned a corner and disappeared from sight. I took a deep breath, exhaled, and headed for the garage.

Chapter 19

Only three skimmers remained in the skimmer garage. I went around to each one and looked inside. Two were four-seaters and the third was a six-seater. I climbed into the third, leaving the gull wing open so Raz would know where I was.

This - my trip to Pode, I mean - was all working out very strangely. I'd thought I was coming here to make a flik, but instead I'd ended up as an investigator, working for the emperor of the largest and most powerful country on the planet. The funny thing was, I was having a great time doing it. I strongly suspected all this was a lot more exciting than making a flik.

Still, I missed Donna. I just didn't miss her as much as I thought I would. I hadn't heard anything from her since the attempted assassination of Emperor Fen had taken me away from Momasu Island, which seemed a little strange. But then, I hadn't attempted to get in touch with her, either. The explanation was simple, really - she was busy playing flik star and I was busy playing investigator.

Anyway, she had Rocket Bomms to keep her company until I returned. Rocket Bomms. I smiled inwardly as I thought of myself being portrayed by an actor with such a stupid name. That couldn't be the name he was born with, could it?

The door at the far end of the garage opened and Raz, accompanied by two guards, entered. He looked around, saw the open door of my skimmer and headed toward me. The two guards followed at a respectful distance.

"Almost ready?" I said to him when he was alongside the skimmer.

"We are ready," he said, speaking Podok. He was carrying a familiar-looking case with him. I'd seen it before, on Earth. At that time it had been filled with weapons. I suspected that might also be true this time.

"Where are the others?" I said.

"Others? What others?"

"The other guards."

"These two are all we need." He turned slightly toward the guards, and they responded, with some difficulty, by saluting me. The difficulty came from the fact each of them was carrying two large laser rifles. Presumably, the extra two rifles were for Raz and me.

I gave them a little wave of my hand, feeling embarrassed as I did so, and said, "Hi, guys." Then I turned my attention back to Raz and said, "Are you sure this is enough? Kiki said Nasty took 10 or 12 officers with him. The four of us will be badly outnumbered."

"Not for to worry, Roger," Raz said in English. Then he turned to the two guards and said, "Come on, let's go. Climb in."

The two guards got into the skimmer, strapping themselves into seats in the back. Raz also got in, taking the pilot's seat, next to me. I pulled the safety harness across my upper body, but because the seats were designed to accommodate tails, I couldn't make it too tight or I'd find myself falling into the tail tube. A sudden stop might prove to be more than a little uncomfortable, but there really wasn't much I could do about it.

"Everybody ready?" Raz said as the skimmer began to hum.

"Ready back here," said one of the guards.

"Roger?"

"Yeah, I'm ready, too. But take it easy, will you? Drive like you're taking your mother to church."

Raz laughed as we lifted off and headed for the PUFF safe house. "Yes, sir," he said. "My mother, Roger." Then he laughed again at his own joke.

"What are we going to do when we get there?" I said.

"First, we'll check it out with a high flyover," Raz said. "Then a low flyover, and then we'll land. But not too close to the house."

"That sounds good. But if the high flyover shows any signs of life, I think we should skip the lower one and just land. If they're in the house, they've probably got guards posted, and they might see us if we get too low."

"Okay, that's good. One flyover and we land."

"You think that's where they went?" I said.

"I hope so. Because if it's not ..."

"Yeah, I know. We're at a dead end."

Only minutes later we were skimming, silently, high above the house the skimmer had identified as the one we were looking for. It was just a couple of miles outside the city limits, but the landscape was remarkably different. We were in the country, and houses out here were separated by large, open expanses - pastures or gardens, was my guess. Or maybe just really big lawns.

"See anything?" said Raz.

"Lights are on," said the guard Raz had introduced to me as Poz. At least, I think he was Poz. For all I knew he could have been Rek, the other guard. Dressed as they were in identical uniforms, they looked enough alike to be twins, and I had already forgotten how to tell them apart.

"See any skimmers?"

"No," said the guard.

"Roger?"

"I don't see anything, either," I said. "Of course, it wouldn't be too smart to leave two or three stolen imperial skimmers in your yard."

"Yeah, they probably hid them or ditched them."

"If that's them," I said.

"Only one way to find out," Raz said. "Let's land and take a closer look." He pointed the nose of the skimmer at the ground and a few seconds later we landed silently in a grassy field a few hundred feet from the PUFF house. The landing was perfect - Raz was getting pretty good at flying skimmers.

Raz grabbed a com from under the skimmer's control panel and his case from under his seat, where he'd stored it. Then the four of us, each carrying a laser rifle, set off across the field, heading for the house.

"What's that for?" I said, pointing at the com.

"In case we need help," he said, and grinned. Raz grinned a lot, it seemed to me. In fact, all Podoks grinned a lot. I wondered if I was misinterpreting the meaning of that look.

We kept going until we came to an area about 30 feet from the house, where a large, leafy tree with multiple trunks - I think it's called a *zodek* tree – leaned out over the lawn. It was here, behind the tree, that we stopped.

"So, what's the plan?" I said to Raz.

"I don't really have a plan," he said. "I'm playing it, as you humans say, by ear. How about you? Do you have a plan?"

"Well, no. But I think we should make sure it's them before we go charging in there with our guns drawn."

"Okay. How are we going to do that?"

"Good question," I said.

"We could take a couple of shots at the house," suggested Rek. Or perhaps it was Poz. "See if they shoot back."

"We could do that," said Raz. "What do you think, Roger?"

"Why don't we just yell at them?"

"Yell at them?"

"Yeah."

"Yell what?" said Raz.

"Oh, I don't know. Something like, this is the police. We have the house surrounded. Come out with your hands up."

"If it's them, they won't come out," Raz said. "They'll just start shooting at us."

"Then we'll know for sure it's them."

"Okay. Let's try it. Who's going to yell at them?"

"I think you've got the loudest voice," I said to Raz. "My vox-box pretty much limits my volume."

"All right. I'll do it," said Raz. He walked over to the side of the zodek tree. "HELLO!" he called. "HELLO IN THE HOUSE. THIS IS THE POLICE. WE HAVE YOU SURROUNDED. COME OUT WITH YOUR HANDS IN THE AIR."

The only answer was silence.

Raz repeated his instructions, louder this time. His voice was so loud there could be no doubt those in the house - whoever they were - heard him. As confirmation, someone inside the house turned off the lights, and the place went dark.

"Must be them," Raz said.

"Or someone else with something to hide," I said.

"So, what now?" said Rek or Poz.

"Well, we told them they were surrounded," I said. "It's pretty much impossible to surround this place with only the four of us, but they don't know how many we are. Maybe, if we spread out around the house, one of us on each side, then we can bluff them into thinking we're a large force, and they'll surrender."

"All right," Raz said. "Poz, you go to the left. Rek, you go to the right, and I'll -"

Both Raz's directions and our plan to surround the house were interrupted by what happened next. Spotlights, mounted behind shields on the roof of the house, were turned on and began sweeping the area around the house on all sides, and several laser shots were fired in our general direction.

"Change of plans, I guess," I said. It would be foolhardy to try to surround the house now, with the entire yard and beyond bathed in light. We were lucky this tree was here to offer us protection. Without it, we would have been caught in the open when the spotlights came on.

"Let me handle this," Raz said.

"How?" I said.

"You'll see." He pulled out his com and made a call on it. I couldn't hear everything he was saying, but I did catch a word here and there - the words 'electricity' and 'grid' came up several times, as did the phrase 'direct order from the emperor.'

"What was that all about?" I said, after he'd disconnected and put the com back in his pocket.

"I'm getting the electricity in this area turned off."

"Oh. Well, that's great. How long will it take?"

"Not long. Not long at all."

Almost as soon as he said it, the spotlights dimmed. They continued to glow for a few seconds, not putting out any appreciable amount of light, and then went completely out, plunging the house, our spot behind the tree and the entire surrounding area into darkness. I had to admire the speed with which the electric company had responded to Raz's request, and at the same time wonder if Raz had a secret word - a secret code word the emperor had given him - giving him the authority to do things like that. Back home, in Hawaii, the same request would have taken weeks of processing and two or three episodes of turning off the electricity in the wrong neighborhoods before it was successfully accomplished. And that was if you were lucky!

"So, now what?" I said. "Go back to our original plan?"

"No. I don't think that will work, now."

"I've got an idea."

"What is it?"

"You see how long the grass is in the yard? It's as high as your waist." This was an exaggeration - the grass was actually about two feet tall.

"What about it?"

"It would be pretty easy to crawl through that grass, all the way up to the house."

"Not that easy," said Raz.

"Why not?"

"Did you ever see a Podok crawl?"

"I can't say I have."

"Well, when we do, our tails stick straight up in the air. You might as well hang a sign on them that says, 'Here I come' or, 'Shoot here.'"

Poz smiled and Rek said, "That's right."

"I don't have that problem," I said. "I could crawl through that grass and no one in the house would see me. It's too dark and the grass is too high."

"And when you get to the house," said Raz, "then what?"

"Yeah, that part I'm less sure of. I was hoping you'd have something in that case of yours. Maybe some small explosive charges. Something like that."

"You want to blow up the house?"

"Not really. But if I could plant a couple of small charges, maybe we could bluff them out by exploding the small charges and then telling them the house is rigged with a big bomb, and if they don't come out we're going to blow the place sky high, with them inside it."

"Oh, that's good. I like that," Raz said.

"So you've got something? Some small bombs or something?"

"Unfortunately, no."

"Oh. Well, scratch that plan, then."

"But I do have a torch."

"A torch, huh?"

"Yes." Raz opened his case, pulled out a small torch, and handed it to me. "You just push this button, here," he said, tapping the button.

I pushed the button and an inch-high flame appeared at the top of the torch. "That's it?" I said.

"That's it," he said. "It's not designed for welding, or cutting metal. It's for starting fires."

"Starting fires, huh? Listen, Raz, do Podok houses burn?"

"Sometimes. It depends on what materials they're made of."

"How about this house?"

Raz looked at the house, which was little more than a dark shadow across from us, illuminated only by cloudy moonlight. "I can't be sure what it's made of."

"Well, what's your best guess?"

"It looks like it'll burn. It's an old house. Usually older houses burn."

"There's our plan, then. I crawl through the grass, set the house on fire, and they'll have to surrender."

"Or come out, at least."

"Yes. And if they don't surrender -"

"Poz and Rek and I will waste them when they come running out."

"I was going to say they'll be in for a hot time, but your way will work, too." I grinned at him and he grinned back.

"You don't mind crawling through the grass?" Raz said.

"I'm the only one without a tail," I pointed out.

"Then I guess it's up to you," he said.

"Besides, you don't have any snakes here in Tetepu, do you?"

"No."

"Good, just like in Hawaii - no snakes. I really don't like snakes." I went over to the edge of the tree and crouched there, surveying the house.

"We do have giant carnivorous worms, though," Raz said as I got down on my hands and knees and slipped into the long grass of the yard. "Watch out for those."

I looked back at him and he was smiling. "Yeah, right," I said, and started crawling toward the house.

Chapter 20

I made my way through the long, slightly-damp grass toward the house, crawling on my belly. Up ahead in the house, Podok eyes were no doubt watching for just such a sneak attack, and knowing that encouraged me to keep my butt down and crawl slowly. No sense advertising my presence.

We should have brought more help with us - if we had, I wouldn't be crawling through this yard, my heart pounding in my chest from a combination of fear, excitement, and exertion. We could have really surrounded the house, and overwhelmed the occupants with the sheer force of our numbers. Of course, it was too late for that now and, as a common expression here in Tetepu goes, *if things were different, then they wouldn't be the same.* I made a mental note to have a little talk with Raz about this apparent desire of his to do things the hard way - by ourselves, with as little outside help as possible.

So I inched my way toward the house, carefully parting the grass ahead of me and then pulling myself forward, into the space I'd just created. The grass itself was exceedingly fragrant, with a mint-like smell that tickled the nose. At least, it tickled *my* nose. Without any warning whatsoever, I sneezed. Loudly.

A volley of laser shots peppered the yard, making small popping sounds as they instantly incinerated pieces of grass around me. I put my head down and waited, wondering how loud a noise I'd make if I got hit. Evidently, this plan of ours - to set the house on fire, thus forcing the occupants out - was not going to be as easy to execute as I'd thought.

As I lay there on the ground of this country, this planet, so far from my home, hoping I didn't get shot, one thought kept running through my mind - how did I get myself into this situation? Just when did I become a hero, anyway? When did I buy into this 'human who saves the lives of Podoks' mystique that had sprung up around me? Heck, I wasn't a hero - I was a teacher.

And yet, I was a hero, even if I was reluctant to admit it. Or, at least, I had been one in the past, and here I was, trying to be one again. After all, I could have spent a nice vacation with Donna, making the flik, but I was doing this instead. Not only was I doing this, I was actually - much of the time, at least - enjoying it.

So maybe there was something to it - maybe it was destiny, or karma, or fate, or whatever you want to call it. Maybe I was born to become 'the human who saves the lives of Podoks,' and being a teacher was just something to keep me busy between exciting adventures.

Or maybe not. Maybe I'd just been lying here in this damp grass for too long, and was getting sappy. How long had it been, anyway? Ten minutes, perhaps? It seemed like hours.

I decided to risk taking a look around. It had been quiet for quite a while - by that I mean no one was shooting at me from the house - so I lifted my head slightly and peeked through the grass.

I needn't have bothered. While I could see the house, which was a white or cream color, and the windows, which were the dark spots on the house, it was too dark to make out anything. Whoever Raz had called to get the power turned off had done a good job. Even though we were just outside the city, there was none of that 'city glow' that shines into the night sky and illuminates outlying areas. The only way that could be was if power to most of Tapu had been turned off.

As I looked around, a dark shape caught my attention. It was to my right, close to the house, tall and thick. It looked like a big bush. Or a small tree.

Whichever, I decided to incorporate it into my plan. I resumed my snake-like crawl through the grass, only instead of heading straight for the house, as I had been, I angled off to my right, toward the bush, moving at a pace that would make a snail laugh. Carefully, I pushed each piece of grass aside and crept forward, one inch at a time. Those in the house who were, no doubt, carefully watching the yard for any signs of movement, would have to have had very good vision, indeed, to have seen me move.

Evidently, that was not the case, because I made it to the relative safety of the bush - which is what it turned out to be - without any more shots being fired in my direction. Once there, I rested briefly, then crawled under the bush and up to the edge of the house. From here, no one inside could see me without sticking his head out a window, something I was counting on not happening.

I pulled the torch out of my pocket, fired it up and got to work, trying to set the house on fire. Immediately, an unexpected problem presented itself. The outside of the house was made of smooth plastic, or some Podok equivalent, and like all the houses I've seen here, it was round. This meant there was nothing sticking out for me to use in getting the fire started - all I could do was hold the torch up against the side of the house and hope the plastic siding would get hot enough to catch on fire. Not having any alternatives, that's what I did. I held the lighted torch up against the house and tried to get the plastic to light.

Several minutes went by. The torch got hot in my hand - so hot I had to pick some grass and wrap it around the torch as insulation. Finally, just when I was giving serious thought to giving up, the plastic began to melt, and then caught on fire.

It wasn't much of a fire - only a couple of inches high and burning so slowly I had visions of Raz and me spending weeks here, waiting for the house to burn down. Still, there wasn't anything I could do about that, so I crawled off toward the opposite side of the house to complete the rest of our plan by setting that side of the house on fire, too. This time, the side of the house offered me protection as I crawled along, and the grass here, close to the house, was much shorter than out in the yard, so it only took a couple of minutes until I'd reached my objective and was hard at work with the torch.

As soon as I had a flame started on this side, I crawled back into the grass and headed toward the safety of the tree, where Raz, Poz and Rek awaited me. I was torn between a desire to go slowly enough so as not to be detected by those in the house, and an equally compelling desire to get out of the yard quickly, just in case the house suddenly erupted into flames, thereby shedding unwelcome light on my position.

As it turned out, my worries about the house bursting into flames were unwarranted. By the time I reached the relative safety of the tree, the flames on the right side of the house were only a couple of feet high, and the flames on the opposite side were less than half that. I started to laugh.

"What?" said Raz.

"Our plan," I said.

"Something wrong is being?"

"Haven't you noticed? It's not working the way it was supposed to. We're not burning them out, we're melting them out."

Raz smiled. "For to have patience, Roger. For to have patience."

"Like I have a choice," I said. I leaned up against the tree and tried to catch my breath. One of these days, I'm going to have to get started on that exercise program I'm always threatening to do, I told myself. A guy my age shouldn't be this much out of breath just from crawling through some grass.

"What happened to Poz and Rek?" I said, noticing for the first time they weren't around.

"Poz is over there to be hiding," said Raz, pointing off to the right. "And Rek is the other side to be covering."

"What about the back side?"

"Also both to be covering."

"They can see the back from where they are?"

"Yes. For to be easy."

When I thought about it, I knew Raz was right. In fact, since the house was round, you really needed only two people - or Podoks, in this case - to surround it. Placed directly opposite each other, each would command a 180 degree view.

Once I got my breath back, I joined Raz at the side of the tree, where he was watching the house, his laser rifle cradled loosely in his arms, ready if he needed it. One unplanned-for effect of the two small fires was to illuminate the house, albeit dimly, while allowing Rek, Poz, Raz, and myself to remain in complete darkness. If anyone inside the house came outside, or stood in a window, we'd be able to see them and, presumably, shoot them.

And that's almost exactly what happened. Someone in the house apparently noticed the growing illumination outside and leaned out a window to see what was causing it. Bad move on his part - Raz immediately shot him. He slumped forward onto the window sill and lay there, not moving.

Unseen hands pulled the injured - maybe dead - Podok back into the house. That was followed by some shouts and loud crashing noises, and then another Podok stuck his head out the window. Raz shot him, too. He pitched forward, through the window, and landed on the ground outside with a thud.

"Nice shot," I said.

"These Podoks are not for to be learning," Raz observed.

The two fires had, by this time, doubled in size, and were putting out a pretty good amount of light. It was beginning to look as if our plan would work, after all, and the house would burn down. It was just going to take longer than we'd expected.

So we waited. Judging by the noise coming from inside the house, panic was beginning to overtake the inhabitants. We heard yells, screams, crashing noises, and several strange, unidentifiable - at least, to me - sounds. Then all was quiet.

We waited some more. Several minutes passed, the tension causing them to take much longer than they usually do. The house continued to burn, and the flames grew larger, but there really was no immediate danger to the occupants.

Still, I imagine, when one is trapped inside a burning house, without any real hope of escape, there must be a strong urge to extinguish the flames. I know that's what I'd try to do. And that's what someone inside the house tried to do. Suddenly, after long minutes of silence, a figure appeared in one of the windows, leaned out and tossed a bucket of water at the flames on the right side of the house. At the same time, another figure duplicated the maneuver on the left side.

Raz and I were caught by surprise. It didn't matter. From off to both our left and our right, the ping! ping! ping! of laser rifles firing filled the night air, dropping the would-be firefighters in their tracks. Poz and Rek were on the job.

After that, it was just a matter of time until the others surrendered, filing out of the house with their hands high over their heads. Five of them, each clad in the uniform of the Tetepuan Defense Force, came out, but none of the five was General Noz-ti Pem. Raz made them lie, faces down and tails up, on the ground, under the watchful eyes and itchy trigger fingers of Poz and Rek, while he and I extinguished the flames at each side of the house, and then searched the inside.

We found three Podoks inside - two of them dead and one slightly injured. Another lay dead on the grass outside the window. None of these four was Nasty Noz-ti, either. The human, or humanoid, was also not present.

Raz used his com to call an ambulance for the injured Podok, then called the police and informed them of what had happened. I was just about to commend him for his enlightened treatment of our prisoners when he grabbed the injured Podok, who'd been shot in the arm, and dragged him into a back room. The door closed with a slam behind them, and I didn't need anyone to tell me what was going to happen next. Raz was about to use his special powers of persuasion to find out what had happened to General Noz-ti Pem.

The noise from the back room was horrible - screaming and thrashing-around sounds like I'd never heard. It went on and on, and then all was quiet. Finally, Raz returned. The look on his face told me he'd been unsuccessful in finding out the location of General Noz-ti.

"No luck, huh?" I said.

"No. He is not to be knowing."

"What about the others?"

"This one is leader being," Raz said. "If he is not to be knowing, no one is to be knowing."

"And the humanoid?"

"Also not to be knowing."

"I see." Much as I hated to concede the fact, it appeared we'd finally hit the dead end which had been threatening this investigation right from the beginning. Nasty had gone off somewhere by himself, and nobody knew where he'd gone. Pretty clever, I had to admit, if only to myself.

Chapter 21

The investigation was over. Well, not over, actually. But it was, as I've already said, at a dead end. None of the Podoks captured at the PUFF safe house had any knowledge of General Noz-ti's whereabouts - he had ordered them to meet him there, but he'd never showed up.

It was just a matter of time until they caught him, though, said the experts. After all, his picture was on every news show, every entertainment show, even on the sides of every tram in Tetepu, always accompanied by the same message - WANTED FOR TREASON, BIG REWARD. Someone was bound to turn him in, they said. There was no place for him to hide.

And so Emperor Fen thanked Raz and me for our efforts on his behalf and relieved us of our investigative duties. We were disappointed - especially Raz, who had really wanted to put Nasty Noz-ti away - but sometimes things don't work out the way you want them to. This was one of those times.

The emperor had granted Raz some vacation time and had ordered us both to 'go enjoy yourselves.' I didn't know what Raz had planned, but my intentions were to return to Momasu Island and resume my vacation with Donna. Maybe, with a little luck, I might even get a small part in the flik.

I was in my room, packing my belongings and cleaning things up a bit, when Princess Sesu showed up at my door, wearing an extremely sad face.

"May I come in?" she said from the open doorway.

"Sure."

She came in and leaned on her tail a few feet away, watching me pack.

"What's wrong with you?" I said. "You look like you just lost your best friend."

"Well, ..."

"Don't tell me. You've got a crush on me again, and you're sad because I'm leaving."

"Well, I am sad, but it's not because I've developed another crush on you. It's just that, ... well, it's always sad to say goodbye to a friend. I'll miss you."

I walked over and kissed her on the cheek. "I'll miss you, too, Sesu. Of all the princesses I know, you're my favorite."

"I'm the only princess you know," she said with a look that was meant as a grin but didn't quite make it.

"Even if I knew a hundred - a thousand - you'd still be my favorite."

"Really, Roger?"

"Yes, really."

If I'd thought I was cheering her up, I was wrong. She started to cry.

"C'mon, Sesu, don't cry. It's not like we're never going to see each other again. I'll be back. And you still have to come to Honolulu and visit me."

"It's not that," she said, dabbing at her eyes.

"Then what is it?"

"I have some bad news for you."

"What is it?"

"Nobody wanted to tell you, but I thought you should know before ... before you go."

"All right, I'm listening. What is it? Is it bad bad, or just bad?"

"It's bad bad."

"Tell me, anyway. Did somebody die or something?"

"I don't want you to be mad at me, or blame me, or think I'm taking any pleasure in telling you this, because I'm not."

"I won't blame you, Sesu. I promise."

"It's about Donna. Miss Cabacungan."

My heart climbed into my throat and threatened to choke me. I struggled to take a breath. "What? What about her? Is she hurt?"

Princess Sesu shook her head, a human habit that had taken widespread hold in Tetepu. "No, no," she said quickly. "She's fine. It's just that ..."

"It's just that what?"

She took a deep breath and blew it out. "She is no longer your sweet patootie," she said.

"What?"

"It's true. She is having a relationship with that actor you told us about."

"Actor?"

"Yes. Rocket Bomms. He portrays you in the flik, doesn't he?"

"Rocket Bomms? And Donna?" I was having a little trouble getting this information to register.

"Yes."

"Donna is having an affair with Rocket Bomms?"

"Yes, that's right."

"How do you know?"

"You know me, Roger. I have my sources. And I thought you should know before you went out there to see her."

I started to laugh.

"You find this information funny?" Princess Sesu said.

"Well, yeah. Think about it. I've been dumped for someone named Rocket Bomms. It doesn't get much funnier than that."

"I thought your heart would be broken."

Now that was funny. Not funny ha ha, but funny strange. My heart should have been broken. After all, I'd just found out my girlfriend, with whom I'd had an exclusive arrangement for nearly two years, was seeing someone else. In other words, I'd been dumped without being notified of the dumping. I should have been sad, or mad, but instead I felt ... well, relieved.

"So you are okay with this news?" said Princess Sesu. "Not upset?"

"I guess so."

"Humans are more complex than I imagined."

"It's like ... my relationship with Donna has run it's course. It was fun while it lasted, but the time has come to move on."

"Will you miss her?"

"Of course I will."

"So now there is no need to pack. You can spend the rest of your time on Pode here, staying with us. My father and mother will be pleased, as will my brother and Raz."

"What about you?" I said.

She flashed those big teeth of hers at me. "I will be the most pleased of all."

"Okay. But I've still got to go out there and see her, and settle this face to face."

"Yes, of course. I understand. And then you will return?"

"Yes. As a matter of fact, I should get going. I'm supposed to meet Raz at the skimmer garage. He's going to fly me out there."

"I'll walk with you to the garage, if you don't mind," Princess Sesu said.

"That's fine." I scooped up my jacket and tossed it over my arm. "Let's go," I said.

"What will you say to her?" Princess Sesu said as we walked side by side down the long corridor leading to the hallway leading to another long corridor that led to the skimmer garage.

"I don't know. Got any ideas?"

"I guess it depends on how you want to handle it."

"What do you mean?"

"You know. You can be angry, you can be slightly upset, you can be unconcerned - there are lots of different ways to handle something like this."

"I'm just going to let it happen - no plans. I'm not going to try to predict the future. We'll talk. I'm sure she'll tell me the truth. Then I'll wish them well and say goodbye."

"That's so romantic," said the princess with a greatly exaggerated sigh.

"Yeah, right. Romantic. That's me."

The skimmer garage finally appeared through a glass door at the end of one of the long corridors. I held the door for Princess Sesu, then followed her through.

"No one's here," she said, looking around.

"Yeah, I'm probably early. Raz and I have trouble communicating time periods to each other."

"That's because you can't tell time."

"Well, on Earth I can. Just not here."

"Whatever. I'm sure he'll show up, eventually. Which skimmer are you going to take?"

"I don't know. Probably the big one. Raz likes that."

We started walking toward the big skimmer, which was on the opposite side of the garage - outside, actually, in the part of the garage that had no roof. About halfway there, I heard Raz's footsteps approaching us from behind one of the skimmers, off to our left. "It's about time, Raz," I said, turning toward him as he came around the side of the skimmer. "I thought you forgot about me."

"Forget about you, Mr. Denton?" said a Podok voice that was definitely not Raz's. "It's not likely I'll ever be able to forget about you, after the way you ruined my plans."

"General Noz-ti?" I said, squinting against the outside light, directly behind him.

"That's right. Hello, Your Highness."

"Don't hello me, you traitor!" said the princess. "You are in big, big, BIG trouble."

"I don't think so," said General Noz-ti. He moved to the side and I could see him clearly for the first time. He was holding a rather large and dangerous-looking stungun in his right hand, and it was aimed at the princess and me.

"How did you get in here?" I said. "Everyone's looking for you. How did you get past the sentries?"

"I didn't have to get in," said General Noz-ti. "I've been here all along."

"What?"

"It's simple, really. Even a human, like you, should be able to understand it. I knew the coup had failed, and we'd lost, long before my men and I fled the palace yesterday. So while everyone else was climbing into skimmers and getting out of here as fast as they could, I got into one, too. The only difference was, I didn't take off. I just sat in there and waited."

"Waited?" I said. "What for? Why didn't you leave when you had the chance?"

"He's a moron, that's why," said Princess Sesu. "He didn't have enough sense to leave when the others did."

"That's not true!" said the general.

"Then why didn't you leave?"

"Unfinished business."

"Hah! I'll just bet. What kind of unfinished business?"

General Noz-ti smiled that oily smile of his. "You two," he said. "That's my unfinished business. You two, and that bodyguard, An-zo. If it hadn't been for you, my coup would have succeeded. I couldn't leave until I saw all three of you dead!"

"That's not going to happen," said a voice from off to our right.

Because all translated Podok speech comes to my ear by way of the tiny, in-ear, vox-box translator, it all sounds pretty much alike to me. Basically, it's impossible for me to tell who's talking without looking at him, or her, and using sight as a means of identification. Despite all this, I knew, without looking, the voice I'd heard belonged to Raz.

I confirmed it with a quick glance to my right. Raz was standing there, slightly hidden by one of the skimmers, and in his hand was a stungun every bit as large and dangerous-looking as Nasty's.

"Well, well, if it isn't the bodyguard," said General Noz-ti.

"Yes, it is," said Raz. "And this is the end of the line for you. You might as well give it up."

"You've got me covered, is that it?"

"That's it, exactly."

"But that's a stungun you're holding," said General Noz-ti. "Even if you shoot me at maximum stun, I'll still have enough time to get off a shot. Maybe two."

"If I shoot you, it will be at maximum stun. Very few survive."

"Hmm. My gun is also set to maximum stun. My plan is to shoot the princess first and then, if I have enough time and coordination left, to take out Mr. Denton. Regardless of what happens to me, that's not going to look good on your job record."

Raz came out from the shadows of the skimmer and moved cautiously toward General Noz-ti. He held his stungun out in front and kept it pointed at the general the whole time.

"Or maybe I'll shoot Mr. Denton first," said Nasty Noz-ti. "I doubt a human could survive a shot at maximum stun, they're such weak, puny creatures. And that way I'll be sure at least one of them dies." He grinned at me as he aimed the gun away from the princess and toward me.

I didn't think much of that idea and said so. "What's the point? You shoot me, then he shoots you - nobody wins. Let's think of a better way, a way where we both come out winners, instead of losers."

"Like what?" said General Noz-ti, keeping that huge stungun aimed right at me.

Sweat began to trickle down my sides from my armpits, and a sudden desire to visit a bathroom came over me. "Uh, how about we let you go?" I said.

"Let me go?"

"Yeah. Just get in a skimmer and leave. We won't stop you and we won't follow you."

Nasty let loose with another one of his unpleasant laughs. "Just like that? Just get in a skimmer and leave? With your blessings?"

"Yes. I give you my word we won't stop you."

Nasty laughed again. "You're missing the point. There's no place for me to go - I'm a wanted Podok, no matter where I go. It's over for me, I've accepted that. I know my life is about to come to an end - probably right here in this garage, very soon - and, well, if that's the way it ends, that's the way it ends. I gave it my best shot, and I failed."

"Then what's all this about?"

General Noz-ti's eyes narrowed and a fierce look came over his face. "About? This is about revenge! This is about which of you three are going to go to hell with me!"

I was still trying to think of something to say that would get all of us out of this situation alive when it happened. With no warning at all, General Noz-ti turned, pointed his stungun at Raz and fired. Seemingly at the same time, Raz fired back. As Princess Sesu and I ducked for cover, I could hear Raz's voice inside my head, saying, in English, "This is not good!" I had to agree.

Chapter 22

Amazingly enough, both shots missed their targets. Nasty Noz-ti failed to hit Raz, and Raz failed to hit Nasty. The two of them stood there, glaring, about 10 or 12 yards apart, their stunguns aimed at each other, each knowing the other would shoot with little provocation. It was, as they say here in Tapu, a Menetian standoff, so called for the citizens of the Tetepuan state of Minetia, who are known for their stubbornness and unwillingness to compromise.

Princess Sesu and I had taken up what I like to call a 'defensive position' behind one of the skimmers. In other words, we were hiding, but watching the goings-on.

General Noz-ti was the first to speak. "So, An-zo, what happens now?"

"You tell me," said Raz.

"One of us has to be the first to shoot again," Nasty said.

"It would seem that way," Raz agreed.

"And the other will have plenty of time to get off a shot."

"Yes."

"So it seems this is the end for both of us."

"Perhaps. Perhaps not," said Raz.

"What do you mean?"

"One of us might miss."

"It won't be me," said Nasty Noz-ti.

"No? Are you sure? You already missed once. What makes you think you won't miss again?"

"I won't. That's a promise."

"It seems a little too easy, don't you think?" said Raz.

"What seems too easy?"

"You know. I shoot you. You shoot me. We both end up dead. Where's the fun in that?"

"Fun? You want it to be fun?"

"Well, maybe fun is the wrong word," said Raz. "But I always envisioned my death as being ... oh, I don't know, more exciting, I guess."

"What difference does it make? Once you're dead, you're dead."

"I suppose."

"And I'm a dead Podok, no matter what happens here."

"That's true. The penalty for attempting to overthrow the government is death. Still, I can't help thinking ..." Raz's voice trailed off.

"Thinking what?" said General Noz-ti.

"Well, you're a military Podok. I can't help but think this will be a disappointing death for you, too. Getting shot by a stungun isn't the same as dying in a glorious battle, for example."

"Do you have something in mind?" Nasty said. "Or are you just stalling?"

"Aren't you a mak su master?" said Raz.

"Yes, I am. You know I am. I've won many tail fighting tournaments and am quite well known for my technique."

"You're right, I've heard of you. I also am a master."

"You? I never heard your name in the mak su world," said Nasty with a sneer. "And I don't recall ever seeing you at tournaments, either."

"Oh, I've been to a couple. Only as a spectator, though. Imperial bodyguards are prohibited from competing in tournaments. We use our fighting skills in real situations, not contests."

"Ah, you're just afraid you'll get hurt, that's all."

Raz smiled. "Yes, that must be it."

"So what did you have in mind? A match? A match to the death?"

"Why not? The ultimate contest."

"What's the point? Even if - I mean, *when* I win, I'll still end up losing."

"Perhaps that's so. But you could have the satisfaction of going out on a high point, knowing you've taken the enemy with you. It seems to me that's the way a real military Podok would want things to end. Of course, ..." Raz's voice trailed away to nothing.

"Of course, what?" said Nasty Noz-ti, who seemed - from my vantage point, at least - to be taking Raz's idea seriously.

"Of course, that's assuming you can beat me. And that's a pretty big assumption."

General Noz-ti laughed that nasty laugh of his - the one that earned him his nickname. "As if there were any doubt," he said. "I don't need to fight you - I know I can knock your tail off. You don't stand a chance against someone with my experience."

"You're not ... afraid, are you?" Raz said.

"Hah!" said Nasty with a snort.

"Because it would be understandable if you were, since all your experience is in tournaments, where they have rules and regulations to prevent anyone from getting seriously injured, and you've probably never been in a real fight - the kind where there are no rules, and anything goes."

"I'm not afraid of you!"

"You should be."

"So you think you're tough, huh?" General Noz-ti said.

"I know *I'm* tough. It's you I have doubts about."

This last remark seemed to do it for Nasty. He lowered his gun slightly and said, "All right. Let's just see which of us is tougher. Put your gun down."

"Not a chance," said Raz. "You put yours down, first."

"Not first," Nasty said. "Together. At the same time."

"All right."

Raz and Nasty, each keeping a wary eye on the other, bent down and placed their stunguns on the floor, then stood back up.

"Now kick it out of the way, so you won't be able to grab it to save your sorry tail, once the action starts," Raz said.

"You kick yours out of the way first."

"Together, then."

"All right. On two, then. Agreed?"

"Agreed," said Raz. "But I'll count."

"We'll *both* count."

"Oh, all right! One - and – two."

"One - and – two," echoed Nasty Noz-ti.

On the count of two, both Nasty and Raz kicked their weapons to the side. Nasty's stungun skittered across the floor and ended up under a skimmer about 40 feet away, directly across from Princess Sesu and myself. Raz kicked his stungun in the opposite direction, toward us. I couldn't see it from my vantage point, but judging by the sound it made as it skittered over the floor, it came to rest a few feet from Princess Sesu.

"Ready?" said Raz.

"Ready," said the general, and added, "Prepare to die!"

The two combatants began to circle slowly, moving closer to each other as they did so. Actually, the word 'slowly' doesn't begin to do justice to the speed at which they were circling. I estimated that, at the rate they were closing the gap between them, it would take 10 or 15 minutes before they actually got close enough to make contact with each other. That just might be the way all mak su matches unfold, or this one might be proceeding at a slower pace because of the high stakes - I wasn't sure. What I was sure about was, at the rate they were moving into fighting range, we were going to be here for a while.

"Can you see the gun?" I said to Princess Sesu. I spoke quietly, not wanting to break the concentration of the two combatants.

"What gun?" she whispered back.

"Raz's stungun."

"It went under the skimmer."

"Can you see it? Can you get it?"

The princess stepped back from the skimmer, keeping her eyes on Raz and Nasty, who were still circling. "I can see it but I can't get it," she said. "It's right in the center and there isn't enough room for me to get under there."

"Okay, I'll get it." I waited until General Noz-ti's back was toward me, then I slid under the skimmer and retrieved the gun, taking only a couple of seconds to complete the task. When I stood back up, with the stungun in my hand, the general's back was still facing me. Raz gave no indication he'd seen what I was doing - his attention was focused entirely on Nasty Noz-ti.

"What are you going to do?" Princess Sesu said.

"I'm going to shoot him, of course."

"Raz won't like that."

"Yeah, probably not."

"He'll take it as a lack of trust in his fighting skills."

"You think so?"

"I know so. He'll think you've lost faith in his abilities."

"It's not that. But what if he does lose? Why take the chance?"

"This will probably end your friendship," Princess Sesu said.

I paused. "I'm in a real bind here, aren't I?"

"If General Noz-ti wins, you can shoot him then. Of course, Raz will be ..." Her voice trailed off, not finishing the thought.

I finished it for her. "... already dead," I said.

"Or, ..." the princess said.

"Or, what?"

"I had a thought."

"Well, tell me. What is it?" Out of the corner of one eye I watched Raz and Nasty continue to circle. They were almost close enough to each other to start making contact.

"*I* could shoot him," said Princess Sesu with as much enthusiasm as she could muster while still maintaining a whisper. "In fact, I'd love to shoot him."

"You?"

"Why not? Raz won't get mad at me - he works for me, for my family. I'll just tell him he's too valuable an employee for me to let him risk getting banged up in some stupid mak su duel. What's he going to do? Get mad at *me*?"

She had a point - being a member of the royal family had its advantages, without doubt.

"C'mon, let me do it. Let me shoot him."

"You're a bloodthirsty little Podok, aren't you?" I said.

She grinned at me. "Please."

"All right. But on one condition - you don't use the maximum stun setting."

The grin disappeared. "But he's big. Anything else might not put him down."

"Then shoot him twice if you have to. But *no* maximum stun. And *no* shots to the head. We need Nasty around to answer questions. He's the only one who knows all the details about this attempted coup - which PUFF members were involved, where the backing came from, who the human was who shot at your father. That sort of stuff. So we need him alive. Okay?"

"All right." She sounded disappointed.

I handed the stungun over to her. "Wait until his back is to us, then just walk over there and shoot him."

General Noz-ti was facing us at the time, so we waited. I was pretty sure we had a foolproof plan - after all, how hard can it be to shoot a guy in the back? If I hadn't thought the plan was foolproof, I never would have let the princess have the gun.

"Now," I said, when Nasty's back was finally turned to us again. "Go shoot him now."

Princess Sesu never hesitated. She walked out from behind our skimmer and headed straight toward Nasty's back, just a few feet away. When she had closed the distance to about five feet, she stopped, raised the stungun and aimed it straight at him.

Perfect, I thought. Or would have thought, if I'd had the time. Because right then, Princess Sesu did something that wasn't part of the plan.

"Hey, Nasty," she said in a loud voice. "Nasty Noz-ti. I'm talking to you. Turn around."

Nasty swung his head around just enough so he could see the princess and still keep an eye on Raz. "Well, if it isn't the spoiled little bitch of a princess," he said. "Come to save your bodyguard, have you?"

Raz started to say something, but Princess Sesu cut him off.

"What did you call me?" she said.

"You heard me."

The general never had a chance. The princess fired. Then, just to be on the safe side, she fired again. And again, and again, and again, and again - six times in all. By the time she was finished, General Noz-ti was a smoldering heap on the skimmer garage floor.

"Look at that," said the princess as I joined her and Raz. "He's smoking."

"This is not good," Raz said to me in English.

"Is he dead?" I said.

"If he's not, it's a miracle," said Raz. He bent down and examined General Noz-ti's body, then stood back up. "No miracles today, I'm afraid."

"Great," I said. "What were you thinking, Princess? You knew we needed him alive."

"I know. And I'm sorry - I didn't intend to shoot him so many times. But did you hear what he called me? I lost my temper."

"No, no," Raz said. "We cannot have a member of the royal family executing General Noz-ti. These sorts of things just don't happen. There will be serious repercussions."

"I'm afraid it's too late," said the princess.

"It's too late for Nasty," I said, feeling little sympathy as I gazed at his body. "But it's not too late for us to ... to get our stories straight."

"What do you mean?" said Raz.

"I mean, no one is here but us. There aren't any cameras here. No one will know what happened, exactly - they'll only know what we tell them."

"You mean we should lie?" said the princess.

"Absolutely not," I said. "We tell the truth - how Nasty surprised us here in the garage, and how Raz showed up, and how he and Nasty started to fight, and how I shot him with Raz's stungun."

"You?" said Princess Sesu.

"Why not? I'm the only one who can get away with it - if it's you or Raz, there will be hearings, maybe even a trial. But I'm the human who saves the lives of Podoks, and I was just doing what everyone would expect me to do."

"You just want the credit for killing him," said the princess, pouting slightly.

"No, Princess, I don't. But neither do you or Raz. This is the best way."

"Why did you shoot him so many times?" Raz said to me. "You knew we wanted to question him."

"Uh ... that was an accident. The stungun jammed. I only meant to shoot him once, but the gun just kept on firing."

Raz looked at Princess Sesu. "What do you think, Princess?" he said.

"Well, I really think I should get the credit - I'm the one who did it."

"Think," said Raz. "Think about all the trouble this will cause your mother and father. Think about how this will affect your popularity with the citizens of Tetepu - after all, you know you're their favorite member of the royal family."

"I know."

"So?"

The princess flashed her teeth. "I think it was darn careless of Roger to shoot General Noz-ti so many times - now we'll probably never find out for sure who was backing him. But I'm also grateful to him for saving Raz and myself from this evil, evil Podok."

"I also am grateful," Raz said with a slight grin.

"Good, then," I said. "It's settled. So let's go tell someone what happened."

Chapter 23

I never did get to go see Donna - what with the commotion caused by the discovery and subsequent death of General Noz-ti, both Raz and I forgot about our planned trip. Besides, I was under temporary detention while Nasty's death was being investigated, and couldn't have left if I'd wanted to. It was just a temporary thing, Princess Sesu assured me, and there was nothing to worry about. I had free run of the palace, but I couldn't leave.

So Donna and I broke up by vidcom. There wasn't much to it, actually. She told me she'd found someone new and I said I understood. She hoped I'd find someone who *really* loved me. I said thanks. She encouraged me to move on with my life. I said I would. She said she'd see me around, by which I guess she meant she'd be coming by my apartment to pick up her stuff, once we both got back to Honolulu. I wished her luck. And that was that - end of breakup.

I was released from detention shortly after my conversation with Donna. Princess Sesu had mentioned to her father I was being detained by his new security staff pending the outcome of the investigation. He became extremely angry, according to the princess, and went to see the new chief of security. Shortly after that he showed up at my room, informing me my detention was a mistake and I was free to do whatever I wanted with the rest of my time on Pode.

The first thing I did was change the arrangements for my trip back to Earth. I was scheduled to go back with Donna, Rocket Bomms, and the rest of the human actors, but I knew that would be awkward for all of us, so I prevailed on Princess Sesu to help me. She got me in with a tour group - 44 Podoks, all from Tapu, plus three tour guides - that was leaving five days earlier than the actors from Earth, on a Maktar ship. They were, according to the princess, 'absolutely thrilled all to pieces' when they heard the great Roger Denton, the human who saves the lives of Podoks, would be accompanying them on their trip to Earth.

I was less than thrilled, knowing I'd probably get stuck showing them around Honolulu, but it's not as if there's a ship leaving every hour, on the hour - sometimes you have to wait weeks to get a flight to where you want to go - so I took it.

The investigation into General Noz-ti's unfortunate demise was also wrapped up shortly after I was released from detention. Although no one ever said anything to me, and I didn't ask, I'd be willing to bet Emperor Fen had a lot to do with that, too. Nasty was written off under the general heading of, 'deserved to die,' and that was the end of that. I wondered if Princess Sesu had told her father what really happened back there in the skimmer garage, but again, I didn't ask.

The other investigation - the one into who, if anyone, was backing General Noz-ti's coup attempt - was stalled. As far as anyone could tell, it was just Nasty and some of his officers, with a little logistical help from PUFF, who were behind the attempt on Emperor Fen's life. Still, there were a lot of unanswered questions about the whole affair, and the suspicion was strong that someone, or some group, perhaps even from another planet, was involved. The fact the human, or humanoid, who was involved in the shooting had never turned up, led many to suspect one of Pode's nearby humanoid-planet neighbors was involved. As far as I knew, though, there was never any evidence to support this - it was all just a strong suspicion. I must admit I toyed with the idea of giving the investigators a call and telling them they should check out an actor from Earth named Rocket Bomms, but I didn't do it and I'm proud of myself for that.

I spent my days sightseeing and working on my books in the palace library. My nights were taken up with a variety of dinners and award banquets given by Emperor Fen and Empress Nememe in my honor. During one of these I was officially *adopted* into the royal family. It wasn't as big a deal as I'd thought it would be - it's more of an honorary adoption than a real one - but I can now call myself Da-mo Denton Roger if I want to, and I have a permanent apartment at the palace.

Usually, after one of these dinners, there would be a party at one of the clubs in Tapu. These were great fun. Princess Sesu would act as hostess, Prince Stee would be the host, and Raz and I would be the guests of honor. There were rock and roll bands, acrobats, contortionists - one party even featured a Podok who could swallow his own tail, or most of it, at least. We'd eat and drink and sing and dance. Podoks - or Podok women, anyway - love to dance, and I was on every fair Podok maiden's dance request list, something I found to be a major chore, because I think dancing is, well, stupid. I much prefer to just sit and listen to the music.

My dancing days came to an abrupt halt one night when a particularly hefty Podok matron stepped on my right foot and broke two of my toes. The royal surgical team reset both of them for me and then, despite my objections, covered my leg, all the way up to my knee, with a gigantic blue and yellow cast. They also made me stay in the infirmary for two days while they poked and prodded me and ran a gazillion tests. I strongly suspected they didn't know what they were doing - after all, Podoks don't even have toes - and were using me to study human physiology, but I couldn't really complain they were treating me too good, so I let them stick me with needles and I answered their questions until they got bored and released me. I guess human physiology wasn't as exciting as they'd thought it would be.

Anyway, the broken toe was, as the old saying goes, a blessing in disguise - whenever some Podok lovely would ask me to dance, I'd just point at my foot and say, "I'd love to, but, ..." and I was off the hook. It also gave me an excuse to miss parties or any other events I didn't wish to attend - I'd just claim my toes were hurting and beg off. Everyone was most sympathetic.

If breaking the toes was a blessing, though, wearing the huge cast was a major nuisance. The palace had been built a small piece at a time, with each generation of Da-mos adding on to it and changing parts of it as they saw fit. As a result, the ground floor was multi-leveled, and I was constantly having to go up six steps in one place and down four steps in another place, just to get around. Because the cast was so big, this was extremely difficult. I put up with it for four days, then went back to the infirmary and had them remove the cast and tape the toes together.

I spent much of my free time with Raz, cruising around Tapu and nearby areas in one of the royal skimmers, sightseeing and meeting 'ordinary' Podoks. Raz took me into his confidence and told me he had already informed the royal family he wouldn't be returning to his bodyguard job after his vacation. He was planning to go into business for himself, as a 'private defective.' I told him at least ten times the word was 'detective,' but he never could keep it straight, and I eventually gave up - if he wanted to be a private defective, well, who was I to stop him?

Raz also tried to get me to commit to quitting my job and joining him in his detective business, but I stalled and made excuses, telling him I'd think about it. He accepted that, but he never stopped talking about how much fun the two of us could have 'cruising the galaxy, helping those who needed our help.' I had to admit, it sounded tempting.

Helped along by four or more hours a day working in the library, my books began to take shape. Actually, that's only half true. One of them was nearing completion - the story of how I met Prince Stee and saved him from kidnappers in Hawaii - but the other one - the history of the Da-mo family - was progressing much more slowly. I was pretty sure I'd need some extra time to finish that.

And then my time on Pode was up. Princess Sesu - the socialite of the Da-mo family - threw one last party for me, at the palace, the night before I was due to leave. It was a grand affair, with dignitaries coming from all over Tetepu to meet me and to thank me for saving their government and to wish me *ma kit po an*. Princess Sesu and Empress Nememe both cried, Emperor Fen called me his 'strange-looking son,' and Prince Stee told anyone who would listen I was his brother. It was, to say the least, a very emotional evening.

The next day, I said my goodbyes to the royal family at the palace. I had arranged - with the help of the palace staff - to board my flight home early, so as to avoid the reporters who were sure to be snooping around, and there really was no reason for any of the Da-mo family to accompany me to the spaceport. Princess Sesu and her mother cried again - I could have predicted that - and even Emperor Fen looked a little misty-eyed. Only Prince Stee held up well, shaking my hand and wishing me a safe trip home.

Raz took me to the spaceport in one of the small skimmers. It was something of a gloomy ride. For most of the trip we were silent, save for Raz pointing out the occasional landmark and me answering with "Uh-huh."

I hate this kind of stuff. Goodbyes, that is. I never can think of anything to say that sounds sincere and thoughtful and truthful. I mean, you can't say what you're really thinking if it's, "Well, thanks for everything, it's been interesting and exciting but I've pretty much had enough of your planet for a while and I can't wait to get back home and sleep in my own bed and get back to my regular life and sure I'll miss you some but goodbye." And then be done with it.

So we went through the motions and did what everyone does when they're leaving - shook hands, clapped each other on the back a couple of times, promised to keep in touch - all the usual cliches.

And then it was time to board. I shook Raz's hand one more time. He wrapped those long fingers of his around my hand and didn't let go.

"This is not goodbye being," said Raz.

"No, of course not. We'll be seeing each other again. Soon."

"Ma kit po an."

"Ma kit po an, min Pode," I replied. "May you live 1,000 happy years, citizen of Pode." I freed my hand from his grip, turned and headed down the tube for the trip up to the interstellar cruiser. I was going home.

Epilogue

I got back to Honolulu with almost three weeks of my vacation still left. I put the time to good use, getting up early every morning and walking down to Waikiki for a swim and some breakfast. Most days, I was back home by nine o'clock, working on my books with my wall, Wally.

In this way I managed to complete the adventure story and to make a significant start on the other book, the history of the Da-mo family of Tetepu. As a matter of fact, the story of my adventures with Prince Stee and Raz will be published early next year, as THE TROUBLE WITH PODOKS. I decided to use a pen name for this book and to use my real name only on my serious, scholarly works. The pen name I chose, Chet Novicki, was the name of a real person - an obscure writer who lived here in Honolulu, about a block up the street from where I now live, back in the 20th Century.

My breakup with Donna didn't have as much impact on my life as I thought it would - guess I was ready to move on. I've seen her a few times since we got back. Things were friendly, but strained, between us - not too surprising, I suppose. The last time I saw her she was getting ready to move to Vancouver, to be closer to the flik industry and, of course, to Rocket Bomms, who lives there. She has hopes of becoming a full-time flik actress. I wished her luck.

So everything was pretty much back to normal, sailing along smoothly, as they say, until a couple of days ago. I was sitting in the Third Planet Lounge, having a beer after work, when a Podok came in, marched right over to my table, leaned back on his tail and, without introduction, said, "I am your help for to be needing, Roger."

That's right, it was Raz. Here in Honolulu. Right in front of me. I almost fell off my chair.

Well, I don't have time to go into great detail here, but Raz is now a private detective, and he's here on Earth to pick up two fugitives in Florida and return them to Sarlanti. One of them is the young daughter of the richest man on the planet, and the other is her boyfriend, an older man who apparently induced the young girl to run away with him. It all sounded pretty ho-hum to me, but Raz assured me he had many, many exciting cases lined up, once he got this rather mundane one out of the way.

And guess what – he still wants me to be his partner. In fact, he was insistent about it, telling me he had already opened an office on Pode and had ordered a huge sign that read, in both Podok and English, *The R & R Premium Detective Agency, Roger Denton, The Human Who Saves The Lives Of Podoks, and An-zo Raz, Guardbody Of The Galaxy, Space Detectives*. How about that? He put my name first. Very considerate.

What could I say? I was flattered. And the whole thing – being a space detective, I mean – sounded intriguing, sounded like something that would fit right in with my newly-discovered enjoyment of excitement and danger. So - surprise! - I agreed.

That's right, I let him talk me into it, right there in the Third Planet Lounge. I might not have said yes were it not for the fact Raz also brought with him some great news for me. Emperor Fen had heard from someone - my bet is on Princess Sesu - about the difference between Pode credits and New North American credits - something he apparently didn't know about - and how the million-credit awards he'd given me weren't worth that much on Earth. He had immediately ordered five million N.N.A. credits transferred into my account. I was now a rich man, a multi-millionaire.

And so, tomorrow, I'm quitting my job. And when Raz leaves to pick up the fugitives and return them to Sarlanti, I'm going with him – to Sarlanti, and then on to Pode, and then on to whatever strange new adventures await us. It looks as if this is the beginning of an exciting new life for me. I can hardly wait to see where all this leads.

Roger Denton
	December 12, 2112 (Earth date)

Please leave a review

Well, this story's over. I hope you enjoyed it. If you did, please consider leaving a review. I certainly will appreciate it, and it will encourage me to write more about Roger, Raz, the Da-mo family and Pode. In the meantime, keep reading for a preview of the fourth book in the series, *The QUEICO Project*. It's a good one.

The QUEICO Project: Podok Tales #4 (preview)

Chapter 1

The first thing I did was quit my job. I mean, a guy can't be galavanting around the galaxy, solving crimes and saving lives, if he's tied to a full-time teaching career. Right? So I quit.

Or rather, I attempted to quit. As soon as I made the decision to partner with Raz in his new detective business – to become, as he put it, a 'space defective' – I scheduled an appointment with Doctors Dennis and David Mortimus, the conjoined twins who were the co-presidents of the Pacific Institute of Technology, my employer.

"The Doctors will be with you in a moment," said the receptionist when I showed up. "Please have a seat." She smiled and indicated the couch across from her desk.

I thanked her and sat down. She continued to glance at me from time to time and smile. Was she hitting on me? Probably not. She was at least 30 years my senior – someone's grandmother, no doubt.

"May I get you something?" she said. "Some coffee, perhaps?"

"No. Thank you, I'm fine."

"All right." She smiled again.

Maybe she was just showing off her teeth. They were amazingly straight and white, and word had leaked out about my interest in teeth.

Or, more likely, she was just being nice. In the past two years or so - during which I had become Earth's leading expert on Pode, Tetepu, and the royal family of Tetepu - people had become nicer and nicer to me. As I became more and more well-known in academic circles, people seemed to like me more.

And they definitely treated me better. Why, just a couple of years ago, it took me weeks to get a meeting with the Doctors, but when I called this time, the receptionist said, "And what time would you like to come in, Mr. Denton?" See what I mean?

My thoughts were interrupted by the receptionist announcing I could go in. She smiled at me again as I walked by her desk.

"You have beautiful teeth," I said.

"Oh, thank you." Her smile got so big it threatened to devour the rest of her face.

"Don't mention it, ... uh?"

"Linguetta."

"What?"

"That's my name. Linguetta."

"Oh. Well, it's ... uh ... very beautiful. Linguetta."

I could feel her smiling at my back as I closed the door behind me. Linguetta. That was no name for an attractive grandmother with nice teeth. It sounded like some kind of noodle. Tiny linguinis, maybe.

"Ah, Mr. Denton. Welcome, welcome," said the Doctors Mortimus as I entered. As they usually did when greeting people, the Doctors greeted me in unison, which gave a peculiar, rich, stereophonic effect. I wondered briefly if they rehearsed that, or if it came naturally.

"Have a seat," said Dennis.

I sat down. Back in the old days, it was difficult to tell the Doctors apart. They were, after all, identical twins. And the way they were conjoined made it look as if they had only one body and two heads that looked exactly alike. So they couldn't even wear different clothes. But about three or four years ago, Dennis got his right ear pierced and put a two-inch gold hoop in it. So Dennis was the one with the earring. He was also the head on the left, when you were facing them.

"What brings you to our office this fine morning?" said Dennis.

"Well, uh, I'm here to resign."

"Resign?" Dennis looked dismayed.

"Resign?" David looked surprised.

"You can't resign," they said in unison. I wish I knew how they did that.

"I can't?"

"No, of course not," said Dennis.

"We need you," said David. "You're the pride of the Institute. You're Earth's leading expert on Pode, and that country there, and that royal family ..."

"Tetepu. That's the country. And the Da-mos are the royal family."

David continued as if I hadn't interrupted. "And you bring great prestige to our small school. We can't let you go."

"I'm sorry, but ... well, I've come into quite a bit of money in the past couple of years, and I don't really need to work, so I've decided to go into business with a friend of mine."

The head on the left – Dennis – leaned forward. "Have you thought this through, Roger?"

"Yes, I have."

"And what is it that you and your friend are going to do? What business, I mean," said David.

"Yes, what could be better than working here?" Dennis chipped in.

"We're going to be ... space detectives." I said it with as much dignity as I could muster, but there's just something about those two words, *space* and *detective,* that, when you say them together, makes it impossible to sound dignified.

"What?" said the Doctors.

"You heard me correctly. An-zo Raz and I are going to become detectives. Space detectives."

The two heads pulled away from each other and attempted to exchange knowing glances, but they were too close to each other and the maneuver was impossible.

"Space detectives ... " said Dennis, rubbing his chin.

"Hmm ... " said David, scratching his head, which, like his brother's, was completely bald.

"Oh, I get it!" said Dennis.

"Me, too," said David, but I could tell from the look on his face that whatever his brother was getting, he really wasn't.

"Get what?" I said.

"This is a bargaining ploy."

"A what?"

"You want a raise. Right?" Dennis said.

"No, that's not it," I said. "I really just want to resign."

"How much?" said David. "How much to keep you?"

"It's not about money."

"But of course it is," said Dennis.

"It's always about money," added David.

"Not this time."

"We'll double your salary," said David.

"Yes, double what you now make, effective immediately," Dennis said. "How does that sound?"

"Well, it sounds just fine, but it won't keep me from resigning."

Dennis looked puzzled. "It won't, huh?"

"No."

"How much, then?" said David. "Would triple your salary keep you with us?"

"No. It's just not about -"

"Four times," said Dennis.

"Five," said David.

"What are you doing?" I said.

"You drive a hard bargain, Roger," David said.

"So, how much do you want, then?" said Dennis. "How much to keep you from resigning? Just tell us."

I could see they weren't getting it, so I tossed out the first big number that popped into my head. "Seventeen," I said, knowing a number that high would end this discussion.

"Seventeen?" Again with the unison thing.

"Yeah, 17 times my current salary. That's what I want."

There was a long, awkward silence, then, much to my surprise, Dennis said, "All right." David nodded in agreement.

"All right?" I said.

"Yes, we agree to your demands," said David. This time Dennis was the one who nodded.

I couldn't believe it. Was I really worth that much to the school? Seventeen time my current salary? I really wanted to quit and join Raz, but a salary that big was tough to turn down.

"Are there more?" Dennis said,

"More?"

"More demands," said David.

"Oh ... oh, yeah. I *do* have more demands."

"We figured you would," said Dennis. He didn't look too unhappy, considering he'd just agreed to pay me a fortune in salary.

"What are they?" said David.

"I don't want to teach any classes, or have to show up for work, or anything like that. I want to have unlimited free time, so I can still go into business with my friend." If 17 times my salary wouldn't kill these negotiations, this surely would.

"No work at all?" said Dennis.

"None?" said David.

"No work at all. None. That's how it has to be."

"How about teaching one three-hour course a year?" said Dennis. "Would you be willing to do that?"

"Yes," said David. "Then we could still list you as a professor."

"You mean, one three-credit course for a whole year? I won't be able to go anywhere if I have to teach."

"No, no," said Dennis. "Not three credits, -"

"Three hours," chipped in David.

Dennis looked annoyed at his brother's interruption. "That's right. You teach one three-hour course, one day a year. That's all."

"Really?" I said.

"Really," said the twins.

"So, let me see if I've got this all straight. I teach a three-hour class – a seminar, I guess – one day a year, and the pay for that will be 17 times my current salary."

"That's correct," said Dennis.

"Effective immediately?"

"Yes, of course," David said.

"Well, this all sounds pretty good for me - what's in it for you?" I said.

"We get to claim you as a professor of Off-World Cultures," said Dennis. "And you won't be able to do any kind of academic work for any other institute of learning."

"That sounds fair," I said.

"Also," said David, "we have right of first refusal on all your academic writings."

"Also fair. But academic writings only. Right?"

"Yes," said Dennis. "You'll still be able to write those adventure stories of yours for whomever you please."

"Great," I said. "And this contract would be for how long?"

"We'll guarantee the contract for as long as you live, provided you live up to the terms," said David.

"One three-hour class a year?"

"Yes," said the twins.

"Seventeen times my current salary?"

"Yes."

"All regular benefits?"

"Of course," said Dennis.

"And a wonderful retirement package," said David.

I couldn't think of any possible situation that would make me want to retire from a three-hour-a-year job that paid almost a million credits in salary, so I nodded and said, "Great."

"It's agreed, then?" said Dennis.

"I guess so."

"Wonderful," said David.

"I do have one question, though."

"What?" said the Doctors Mortimus, looking alarmed.

"Why are you doing this? Agreeing to pay me all these credits for hardly any work at all. What's in it for you?"

Once again the heads of Dennis and David Mortimus attempted to exchange meaningful glances, and once again the result was failure. They turned their attention back to me.

"Can you keep a secret?" said Dennis. "A really big secret?"

"I think so."

"It's important. We really need to know. And be truthful," advised David.

I briefly pondered the question. It presented me with a moral dilemma. I've always considered myself to be an honest person, but, and it's a big but – two buts, actually – I am both extremely poor at keeping secrets and, at the same time, an extremely curious person. Especially about secrets.

"I'm sorry," I said. "I got a little distracted, thinking about the size of my new salary. What was the question?"

Both brothers smiled, and said, "Can you keep a big secret?"

"Oh, sure," I lied. "I'm really good at keeping secrets."

Dennis lowered his voice to a near-whisper, as if he were afraid someone might overhear. "We're positioning the Institute to become a major player in Intergalactic Studies."

"That's right," added David. "Over the next couple of years, we'll be adding some new, very important people, to our faculty. People who will greatly increase the prestige of the Institute – along with you, of course. And then -"

"And then," said Dennis, taking over from his obviously-irritated brother, "we go public."

"Go public?"

"A stock offering, Roger," said David.

"An IPO," said Dennis.

"I see."

"Of course, we'll work some options into your contract, if you'd like," said Dennis.

"You'll make a fortune," said David.

"That's great. You can't have enough credits," I said, but even as I said it, I had my doubts as to the veracity of that statement.

The Doctors Mortimus rose from behind their desk, signaling the end of our meeting. I stood and shook hands, first with Dennis and then, left-handed, with David. "We'll prepare the contract," they said in unison.

"Fine."

"Everything will be effective immediately," said Dennis.

"We'll let you know when it's ready," said David.

"Okay." I backed my way out as the Doctors waved goodbye.

Outside the office, the receptionist – Linguetta – was still smiling. I had a smile on my face, too. After all, I'd just negotiated a deal that would pay me nearly a million credits a year for three hours of work. Not that shabby.

"Did everything go okay, Mr. Denton?" said Linguetta.

"Oh, yes. Better than okay, actually."

"I'm glad," she said.

"Let me ask you a question," I said. "I know why I'm happy, but why are you so happy?"

"I'm happy for you, of course. I'm happy you'll be making such a huge salary."

"You are? How do you even know about that? Is the office bugged or something?"

Linguetta giggled. "No, of course not, silly." She leaned forward and lowered her voice. "I knew about it before you did."

"No."

"Yes." She nodded her head vigorously. "I know everything that goes on around here."

"I'll bet that's true. But what, exactly, did you know before I got here?"

"Well, I knew you were planning to resign."

"You did, huh?"

"Yes. Of course, it was just rumors. No hard facts."

"Of course."

"And I knew the Doctors were going to offer you two million credits a year to stay and teach at least one class."

"What?"

"I knew the Doctors -"

"No. I mean, how much? What was that figure?"

"Two million a year," she said with a big smile.

"Two million, huh?"

"Yes. You're going to be – I mean, you *are* a rich man."

I thanked Linguetta and exited the office. So the Doctors had put one over on me by getting me to agree to a contract that paid less than a million credits a year when they were prepared to pay me a lot more. I suppose I should have been really upset – maybe even angry – but I wasn't. Basically, I already had all the credits I'd ever need, thanks to the generosity of Emperor Da-mo Fen, and any extra from the Pit would be just, just ... what's that ancient expression? Gravy on the cake? Yeah, that's it. Any extra would be just gravy on the cake.

As I walked from the administration building to the parking lot, I started to whistle. To hell with credits – they weren't the most important thing in this situation. Not by a comet's tail. This was something that, to me, at least, was a lot more important than credits. I was going to be a space detective!

*****

Wow! A space detective, huh? That sounds, . . . interesting. Too bad that's the end of the preview. Roger and Raz's first case together turns out to be a pretty exciting adventure. To read more, grab a copy of *The QUEICO Project: Podok Tales #4* from your friendly online bookseller.

If you have time and you haven't already done so, please leave a review. Reviews help independent authors like me get noticed among the 18 billion other books available at online bookstores (a polite way of saying reviews help sell books but don't say I'm the one who told you – it's supposed to be a secret).

Thanks for reading.
Chet